THE PRESIDENTIAL MONARCHY

Cuauhtemoc Gallegos

Merl Publications
Orlando, FL

AUTHOR
Cuauhtemoc Gallegos

EDITING CONTRIBUTORS
Victor Colotla
Linda Sue Hayes

COVER
PORTADA
Eric Gallegos
Fadia Tamer

Publisher's Cataloging-in-Publication data
Names: Gallegos, Cuauhtemoc, 1946-
Title: The Presidential Monarchy / by Cuauhtemoc Gallegos
Description: a First edition paperback| Orlando, FL: Merl Publications, 2021.
Identifiers: LCCN:2020906378 ISBN: 978-1-886347-08-3 (softcover)
Subjects: LCSH: Prose fiction | Political Novel | Historical Novel | BISAC: FIC 037000
Classification: LCC: PN 3441 | DDC: 813

Website: www.merlpublications.com

INTRODUCTION

It was 1968 when I last wrote about Mexican social issues, now after more than fifty years, it is my intention to write again, this time to share about my personal experiences to new generations. However, I soon realized, that the main topic of my writings has had already being done by others, and the facts surrounding the massacre of the Mexican people by a group of soldiers under the express orders of President Gustavo Díaz Ordaz and Secretary of the Interior Luis Echeverría Alvarez at the *plaza de las tres culturas* was well established.[1]

That is why I have now, without the pain that has affected me for so long, decided to persist on my desire to put down on paper my ideas and to write about what I have experienced. The first subject I addressed was the history of Mexico after the 1910-1917 revolution. This topic forced me to be as objective as possible when carrying out the corresponding research. I had to conclude, however, that the revolution and the actions of the group in power did not benefit the majority of the Mexican people.

Once completed, this investigation revealed that the period from the end of the revolution to the year 2000 in Mexico refers to the history of a government formed by a small group of individuals who deceived the Mexican people seizing much of the country's wealth and public services and giving it to a little more than 20 percent of the population in 1960, and no more than 30 or 40 percent in later years.[2]

[1] See per example, Memory and History of Mexico '68, por Eugenia Allier Montaño (UNAM), in Revista europea de estudios latinoamericanos y del Caribe = European review of Latin American and Caribbean studies, October 2016, www.researchgate.net/publication/309161036_Memory_and_History_of_Mexico_%2768 or in JSTOR. Tlatelolco 1968 in Contemporary Mexican Literature Introduction by Victoria Carpenter in Bulletin of Latin American Research Vol. 24, No. 4 (Oct., 2005), pp. 476-480. In https://www.jstor.org/stable/27733801

[2] This percentage, being an estimated figure, has been calculated using two different methods: first, estimating that all poor people from the total population in 1960 was approximately 80% (using statistics by Miguel Székely); Second, it was also estimated by including all those people belonging to political corporate groups plus the majority of military personnel receiving similar

Due to this government's group neglect and abandonment of the country's rural areas, a large wave of farmers emigrated to the cities with the expectation of better salaries, opportunities for higher education and improved access to health services that were unavailable to them in the countryside. Starting in the eighties, this vast number of persons had fully arrived in the cities and had begun to greatly influence every aspect of these larger urban communities.

Without pretending to study in depth the major problems of Mexico, in examining its recent past it is evident that major errors were committed by the national government after the Institutional Revolutionary Party, PRI, was formed. The development at the end of the Mexican revolution of a rigid official party and presidential institution established an authoritarian and monopolistic system to solve political and economic problems which prevented these entities from developing the necessary flexibility to adapt to changes in the social environment of the country and the world.

As an inevitable result in the end both the official political party and the presidential institution adopted an antagonistic attitude against Mexican society. In addition, as if this were not enough, some Presidents greatly contributed to this ill will with their pretensions of being great statesmen, which they were not, and at times simply with their greed and personal corruption.

In Mexican history there were great hopes for material advancement after the revolution and the promise of major economic development during what became favorable conditions worldwide. Unfortunately, the rigidity of the political institutions as well as the Presidents who did not allow the country to take advantage of such a clear opportunity, stunted the country's growth, and led to its missing out on what could have been a great achievement.

Mexico's population grew to such an extent that the Partido Revolucionario Institucional (PRI) that was in charge of running the government and had been stimulating its growth, stopped doing so. The crisis resulting from the immense human wave that landed in the cities, was left for other governments to address after damage had been done. Regrettably the PRI government is also guilty of a most inept management of national

services and private rich individuals as well (for a total of 7.7 millions of individuals in 1960). As indicated on the supplemental statistics (p. 117), the poverty index was reduced little by little, until 1998, when increased again, only to be reduced in later years, but still remaining high.

resources, when additional oil wealth was discovered in the eighties and instead of using it to benefit the people, its legitimate owner[3] was given to foreigners and high public officials.

There is no doubt that the country will overcome its recent past and will find a better future. Before that can happen, however, it will have to clearly declare who has harmed it and how. It is in this spirit that this novel starts to travel the rocky path towards the truth. Surely, criticism of individuals with specific interests will lessen the influence of this book, but it is my intent, from someone who should have died in the *plaza de las tres culturas* to add a voice on which to build the truth.

Even though this novel refers in detail to the facts and progress corresponding to recent history of Mexico, their appearance in these pages, more than anything else, serve to support the narrative following the main character of the story. Of course, the script of the novel is totally fictional and was created for the sole purpose of permitting the reader to identify himself with the main character.

Mention of historical events, as well as the interspersed and supplementary statistical tables are factual and, above all, are intended to corroborate what the characters say in the novel. Should any reader consider that some or much of the data are incorrect, said reader should keep in mind that what is being said or assumed by the characters in the novel is based on the indicated sources.

Finally, the interpretation made of recent Mexican history is my personal point of view, after observing the country from abroad for a long time, and although I sincerely believe that it is an accurate interpretation, I also believe that the historic division between liberal and conservative forces still exists and is alive in the country, and until that dichotomy is resolved Mexico will not be able to access and attain the rank of a developed and progressive country.

I want to thank many persons for their help during this investigation and writing of this small literary work, especially the editors and reviewers who without any particular interest nor compensation read the draft of my book. I especially, want to thank Carlos and Lourdes Colotla who offered their home and their warm friendship in Mexico City, my always dear friends, Victor Martínez, Ramón Torres Solís and my brother in law Victor Colotla who all

[3] See Lopez Portillo's obituary in The New York Times on February 18, 2004, by Jonathan Kandell.

contributed great comments. It would not be possible to publish this book without mentioning *señora* Evangelina Valdez, my landlady in Zapopan, México, during several months, including part of the coronavirus pandemic period. In addition, it would have been impossible to publish this book without the participation of my son Eric Gallegos, my friend Fadia Tamer, both from Chicago, and Linda Hayes from Orlando, Florida who undertook the final English review, all of them from the United States of América. Similarly, I also wish to recognize the following top educational institutions that gave me access to their libraries:

The Public Library of the City of Vancouver, British Columbia, in Canada. The Public Library of the City of Chicago, Illinois. The Library of the University of De Paul in Chicago, Illinois. The Library of the University of Loyola in Chicago, Illinois. All of these located in the United States of America.

The Library at El Colegio de México and Libraries at the Law and Economy Schools of Mexico's National Autonomous University (UNAM) in Mexico City, Mexico. The Library of the Centro Universitario de Ciencias Economico Administrativas (CUCEA) and The Library of the Centro Universitario de Ciencias Sociales y Humanidades (CUCSH) both from the Universidad de Guadalajara (U de G), in Guadalajara City, Jalisco, Mexico.

I

"I did not come to see if I could, but because I could I came"
Popular saying.

Toño did not really recall when they all began the great march, that significant moment when moving to the capital changed their lives forever. He had been too young to remember. It was Don Gabriel, the old and almost patriarchal figure who made the monumental decision that his family of farmers should leave their desolate and barren lands. Toño was always fascinated to hear others recount how this fateful decision had come about.

He would ask the elders to tell him again and again how this march took place and, standing silently, he would hear someone say: "when the lands belonging to your family suffered one of the worst dry seasons they had ever seen, Don Gabriel, who was nearing a very old age, had a vision of the fate and future of his people, which would normally be confused with wisdom. He knew that they had reached a crossroads, a moment of decision that pushed them forward and forced them to leave and seek another way of life. Future generations would thank him for having made this decision at a crucial moment, but now it was necessary to leave behind everything they had known for so long and that had provided them with security. It was time to take along everything useful and to undertake the long march, which he himself might not finish, it was time to start the march that would take them to a different, but better life."

It was then, the elder telling the story continued, that Don Gabriel stated the most important words of his life: "Why can't we? I am sure it can be done. In the capital there is enough wealth. We are Mexicans. Why in hell should we die from hunger on the piece of land we were born on? No, those sons of bitches who have taken everything away from us have even more than they need, and it will be enough even for us. To the capital we are going, and it will not be to cause pity."

"His word was the law. So all of them, without even thinking about it, were ready to leave the shady mud house which had been their shelter and the only home they have ever known. Even more important, they also abandoned the large piece of land that depended on the rain and which was now dry and desolate. Left behind was the garden plot next to the house from which the family had barely nourished themselves these last years. Left behind was the village where sometimes they would buy things they needed and whose inhabitants were neighbors and close friends with whom they shared sad moments and happy times. Left behind was the past and its memories. The future was here, the time to go to the capital had arrived."

Toño thought about his original family and of Don Gabriel, dead some time ago, during the first years after they emigrated to the city – that group of impoverished peasants he had dearly loved in the past. He recalled how, little by little, they formed part of the multitude of people called "city", that generated occupations available to anyone with a true desire to survive; how all of them, some with help and others without it, were part of the gigantic body making up that great assemblage; how he had initially worked in an upholstery shop and; how, after forcing himself to attend lectures in school, he had reached the conclusion that he would never be considered an important and honest person without a full education.

Though he was not the only educated person in his family, he was the most rebellious and discontent. All the others were soon satisfied with a normal middle-class life, some were even lucky enough to have greater income and to be considered part of the country's upper-class. But not Toño, his ambition was not to accumulate awards or money, but to acquire the understanding of the truth. In the case of the society in which he was living, his highest ambition was to understand the reality surrounding him and of the city where he lived. All these ideas were embodied in a concerted effort to study and surround himself with like-minded people. Soon, almost without realizing it and being almost thirty years old, he landed in the Mexican bureaucracy where he had to use his many personal talents, such as his good sense of humor, his keen insight, and his shrewd skill in finding out who was in power.

On his first day, Toño thought that day that the federal government offices were going to be filled with people and activity even at that early hour, but upon arriving he found the offices almost empty. Soon the employees occupying the offices started to arrive, slowly filling the room. An hour later the group that had recently arrived seemed to have grabbed all the available places and one could see many people hurriedly moving from one place to the next and especially moving towards the offices located at the end of the huge room, which were wide cubicles with solid walls and wooden and glass doors. The bureaucratic heads occupied those offices, where they dispatched their affairs behind a disorganized pile of papers placed on top of the desk in the center of the room.

It would be years before Toño would occupy one of those offices. It was only after his exceptional ability as an analyst was recognized that his good friend Anibal, who was already the head of a group, recommended him for a more demanding position. The office next to Anibal's had been empty for a long time, due to the unexpected death of its occupant, and that was the place that Toño received temporarily and on probation. Several years later that same office was still his, temporarily and on probation. However, there was no doubt about his qualifications as a leader and his skill as a bureaucrat who should be in the upper echelons of the government.

His next steps in climbing up the ladder of power were neither easy nor free of corruption. To a large extent his climbing up was eased by his friend Anibal, who being a classmate of one of the possible future presidential candidates, brought him along to his new assignment in the federal Ministry of the Interior. It was there that, after having arrived as a mere analyst, he became a major element in the formation and compliance of every State of the Union's financial budget.

When Anibal appointed him to be a member – and naturally an important bureaucrat of the federal Auditing office – Toño was not greatly surprised at his transfer from a mostly political to a mostly technical government agency. However, as time went by it was clear that Anibal had wanted to place him in a position where he could obtain confidential information, since he trusted him, but not so close as to be included in the team joining the possible candidate to the Presidency, should his candidacy be more than a mere possibility. Time went by without much commotion, but suddenly and without any previous notice, Anibal's friend became an actual candidate. It was then that Anibal's friendship seemed to change drastically: he was not as available as before, and he no longer wanted to know details of the accounts in the Auditing office nor which politicians were having problems with a pending audit in the federal office where Toño worked. Slowly his friend became more distant and almost a stranger who would ask, through a formal request, for information on a specific tax payer that he could now get from other channels. Toño preferred to look for a group of friends that better reflected his preferences and above all his moral values. Thus, his friends were reduced to only a few people and even fewer close coworkers.

At that time, the most important bureaucratic personal quality was to have a personality that invited the trust and confidence of others. Thanks to that, Toño had developed lasting and loyal friendships that allowed him to climb the bureaucratic hierarchy, little by little, until reaching the top. His talent for inspiring confidence was of great help, but in no way could be determined as decisive. Friendships made in the past, especially in the classrooms, were perhaps the most important criteria. Among these Anibal was the most important, but others also helped him climb the steep government ladder.

Outside of the workplace, Toño preferred persons with similar ideas and only as an exception someone who held opposite points of view. His ideas were simple and practical according to him: everyone was equal and should be treated as such, everyone was an individual, and everyone shared the same personal objective – the wellbeing of their families and close friends. However, in México, especially in the political arena, important people were willing to take advantage of others if they had the opportunity, or to insult, humiliate or abase others if necessary. In that world, it was said, you could take advantage of those who show any type of reverence towards you. On the other hand, you had to suffer insults and follow orders from persons who, without being superior, held a higher hierarchical position. For Toño it was not necessary to take advantage of anyone nor to suffer insults, since they all were his dear friends and his equals.

His ideas were certainly straightforward, but also contradictory. To take advantage of another person due to their reverence or to be able to humiliate someone when holding a superior position meant that they were not equals in the end, but in the real world they were for him. More than once he had had to point out his stand, asking a subordinate not to ingratiate himself by doing him a favor or rendering free service. Equality has never been a Mexican concept; even today it does not exist in Mexican society. It is customary and necessary to keep social inequality alive. Nevertheless, cultural differences between subservience and inferiority are frequently confused. It is typical, for example, to treat members of the indigenous population as inferior who do not belong to Mexican society for being different and for having a world-view that is not included in traditional Mexican culture. Even though the revolutionary governments have made a great effort for a long time to consider them a part of the nation, the magic formula to integrate them into the national culture has not yet been found. In any case, Toño treated all his friends without prejudice nor special consideration, it did not matter whether he had met them yesterday or long ago. In fact, he preferred that they have a recent history in the city, like his. He was not ashamed of his arrival to the capital, or of his efforts to find sustenance and compassion. Although his feelings were slowly fading due to the harsh and inhumane discord of the city, he tried to keep them alive and in the open. He would still tear up when raggedy beggars or shabby old women would beg him for a handout. His coins were always welcome in the miserable neighborhoods of the city.

Toño was especially angry when mandates and humiliations were handed out, he had always thought that intelligence and understanding were better motivators than orders and force. Still according to the successors of the revolutionaries, Mexican society, especially old post-revolutionary society understood force better than persuasion.

II

"When in bad weather, show a brave face"
Popular saying.

Attending a school of higher education was almost a dream almost impossible to phatom. Fortunately, Toño had an excellent memory which allowed him to stand out in his rural elementary public school, and soon he was competing with other farmers who, like him, had come to the city. His family demanded his greatest effort, and he was willing to give it in exchange for allowing him to study. Soon he learned enough to find a job and in exchange for working, he asked to continue in school. It was evident that learning for him was limitless and no one was going to stop his efforts. When he finally stopped studying (if he ever did), he had two doctorate certificates, one in law and another in economics, and an extensive knowledge of the social sciences.

As far as the law was concerned, his position was that in order to work every society needs compliance with a structure of norms; nevertheless, there are several norms that are by definition not legal, but political, and should be created following political procedures. He would come to believe that expanding litigation and the judicial reach to most social areas was a mistake. On the one hand, in a country like the one he lived in, the practice of ignoring legislated rules should stop; on the other hand, norms should be legislated based on the existing reality. As far as the economy was concerned, the conclusion of the economic sciences was that these sciences had not yet reached levels of practical operation. Consequently, their recommendations should always be subordinated to practical criteria and to other more advanced social sciences. The current economic criteria could be applied to Mexico, but only when properly adapted to the real conditions of the country.

These conclusions and many others, as well as Toño's broad knowledge, would make him especially valuable in practical organizations, such as the government, where his points of view were followed in spite of his somewhat unorthodox opinions. When he started working in the government, in 1997, Toño did not impose his viewpoints. However, as events confirmed them, his coworkers pointed out his acumen and knowledge and he was eventually elevated to a leadership position. This also thanks to his pragmatism and his friendship with Anibal, at that time one of the most important members of government in economic matters.

While his pragmatism was born from his conviction in his studies, his friendship with Anibal came from being classmates in economics classes at the university. Anibal was older than he was and had earlier met many important politicians. When one of Anibal's close friends was postulated to be President of the country, Anibal not only supported him, but put all his personal time and money into his candidacy. On the day of the election he spent countless hours altering the results of the race that his candidate, being the official party candidate, would win anyway, as was customary in Mexico.

Occasionally, Toño would think about his difficult and exceptional journey that had allowed him to jump from being a mere farmer in the countryside to becoming an important bureaucrat. And then he wondered how many had achieved it as well. And the answer was obvious, almost no one. The point was not to think of himself as exceptional or unique, but to ask himself why not more? The answer was clear: because the societal structure did not allow it, because that is not supposed to happen. The obvious answer to such a question was that society should change, and Toño as an example of what was not supposed to be, was committed to its implementation. That was one, if not the most important reason for his presence in the federal government.

But how can you change a society anchored in the past and with an imperceptible movement forward? It can only be changed very slowly, when most of its members decide to do it themselves. The government can exercise its leadership role and be the spark for such change, but nothing can be done if the population is unwilling to change. Even without the participation of the government or politicians, the first step should be to convert the inhabitants into people who adopt certain minimal standards of modernity. From these, other changes would arise that would modify society forever. Without knowing it, Toño thought, in the case of Mexico the federal government has helped achieve the first step: people are now urban, they are no longer illiterate and they think that health and education are important. Everything else will arrive on its own, in spite of idleness and corruption.

Little by little all of his other relatives had settled into the urban society they were destined to live in. Almost no one remembered their humble origins, many of them were now elbowing with persons of lineage and better born. But not Toño, who in spite of his academic distinctions, never stopped considering himself a rural day laborer who was doing better now. "That is the way the revolutionaries must have felt. Most of them came from the countryside and were illiterate day laborers who by using their weapons and their guts, made their condition equal to that of others," he used to say.

"After all, we are all equal" he would like to add, with the conviction of someone who knew it was true. Never before the doors of society had been opened for those with ability or desire and preferably with both. But there are elements, nevertheless, that hinder society's progress, never before the message had been given to the youth that living was an exercise in dependence and of lack in originality and independence like today. In addition to this wrong education, cultural beliefs invade all society. "However, it is true that there are no obstacles now to go from being a street vendor to being a government employee. Finally there seems to be equality, or almost," he would add.

Toño truly believed in the arrival of the populace in the cities of Mexico, and many statistics supported him. Never before there were as many schools of higher studies as today, never before the illiteracy rate was as low, never before the primary schools had their classes full of children and young people eager to learn and to get ahead in their desire to occupy an important place in society.

Toño felt part of an overwhelming wave formed by all those young people seeing everything differently, as if the past had never existed. In a way, the new generation should expect everything to be new, without past compromises, as if starting from scratch. But what happened in the past could not be completely erased; there was a need to keep remnants from the past that could be useful and that could now guide the new generations. In social and economic matters, the country had advanced and had made important choices, though some were shocking and plainly wrong. But it was now up to the new generations to accept what was done and to correct the course. Extreme liberal capitalism did not seem to be the path everyone preferred to take in economic matters. Social inequalities were so great that a different approach seemed necessary. Mexican political corporatism had been destroyed but its substitute was not yet in sight. "If at least this great wave of people could give us some of its answers now," thought Toño.

The nation, and Toño concurred, was at a moment of decision.

III

"No one learns from inside someone else's head"
Popular saying.

Toño questioned the composition of the Mexican society. Not that he had not done it before, but for the first time his answers were different. It was the first time he realized that society was divided into those that had everything and those that had almost nothing. Those who had everything were a small privileged minority, that – for decades had pretended to have special status. The great majority, however, had finally started to move towards seizing the political power that would necessarily change the policies that were being followed, and thus, the distribution of wealth in the country.

Toño thought about his origins, his sacrifices and achievements, and his family. He and his family belonged originally to the group of the dispossessed, poor farmers bettering themselves through their own efforts and through those of their companions in their strange trip. They were now part of the Mexican bourgeoisie and their duty, as good government soldiers was to strengthen their privileges and to defend their achievements before the threatening majorities. But he knew well that his effort would be useless, if not right away, soon. In a not so distant future the armies of the majority would topple the sand castles built to defend their pretentious minority, transforming society into something more egalitarian, sentimental and fair.

He still remembered, vividly, how after arriving to the city when they had first sheltered themselves in the metal-sheet shack at the edge of the city, his friend, the aspiring politician had allowed them to squat on a small piece of land where they could build a small structure and then pay him later. The payment threatened to become a monthly bribe, but between intimidation and his friend's disappearance, it ended up being a one-time payment made in advance to someone unknown who happened to have the property deed. The structure grew and became one of many half-built houses under the expert advice of Don Cleto, the construction worker most popular in the brand new neighborhood. The house grew larger thanks to contributions from everyone in the family and soon it became a really big house from where all its inhabitants departed to every part of the city. Toño missed the half-built construction, with concrete joists made of half-poured concrete, walls of unplastered red bricks and the kitchen's uncaulked tile floor. He missed the smell of damp cement and the pleasant company of his nephews and nieces jumping and catching small animals in the left-over rain, which became a puddle of watery mud, in the small rectangle outside in front of the house, that one day would become a garden lot.

Life in the city had transformed Toño's way of being, talking, and seeing things. The country had been left behind and his family, who he had witnessed grow and change, was a group that with difficulty could be told apart from other groups in the city. Their clothes, their appearance and their manners now belonged to city people. But even more important, their way of seeing society and reacting to it was not from the country anymore. They were still excited about attending a rodeo show where some horse acrobatics were performed and country pride was extolled, but apparently the city was far more interesting and better. It was customary to go to the cinema and to invite friends to gatherings on Sundays, which ended up being parties with dancing and more. Even though the family was finally scattered, their connection and emotional closeness was never lost. All three of his brothers started their own activities and used their intelligence and imagination, in an environment that allowed them to become important and respected persons. His three sisters had married good men and formed their own families. But Toño was still single and in love with knowledge. During one of his many lectures he met and became intimately attached to Rachel, another soul in love with the mysteries of life. He believed that one day he would marry her, although it was not necessary nor did it seem appropriate now. His life was already sufficiently busy and full of obligations to add one more. At this time, Rachel probably hoped to marry and start a family but for Toño it was not the right time. Toño's family soon evolved, becoming an unrecognizable group. They now frequently attended symphony concerts, theater and even opera, though the most important event was always the Sunday family debate around a fashionable topic. Those great debates always changed but also taught everyone how to reason and to debate, which was a clue to the personal success of all.

Toño still remembered the great debate around global warming. It was at the beginning of these gatherings that the topic was addressed, and although the Paris Agreement had not yet been signed binding every country in the world to reduce earth's temperature by under 2 degrees centigrade, discussions were memorable and decisive for all participants.

The initial premise was that global warming was real and that every country could be affected should the earth's temperature be allowed to increase as predicted. It was argued that two-thirds of such increase was due to carbon dioxide (CO_2) in the air, mostly because of industrial development. Even though this premise was clearly accepted, discussion took place regarding the possibility of an accelerated decrease, especially referring to those countries that most contributed to the creation of greenhouse gases.

These discussions led to the conclusion that the ways of using energy in the production of consumer goods was not viable in the long run, a conclusion contrary to the current objectives of most industrial corporations, which led oil companies to reject most international agreements on these matters. The clear purpose of most industrial and oil companies, as well as governments that were affected was to delay the implementation of measures aimed at global temperature reduction. Unfortunately, even those measures were considered very modest, taking into account the actual advance of global warming.

The necessary change of the industrialization process is a topic that has not been considered in most countries and which seems impossible to achieve. Would it be possible to substitute the traditional sources of energy? It did not seem to be the right solution in the time available to control global warming, yet it seemed to be the position many countries had adopted.

What would be the behavior of humanity now when confronted with this great dilemma? Even though there are truly some people convinced of the benefits of a full understanding of the actual situation, concrete measurements are difficult to take; moreover, in some cases to be able to execute them implicates the industrial disintegration of entire industries, not to mention entire societies. It is due to those considerations that it was concluded that there is a natural reluctance to the adoption of measures aimed at decreasing global warming, but on the other hand, it is a matter of generational responsibility that most current inhabitants are not willing to accept. Many countries, in view of the current situation, have engaged their actual populations in some measures to reduce production of harmful gases, when the problems refer to what is going to be given to future generations. Solutions to the continuity of the planet's habitability are not going to be solved now, among other reasons, because existing generations do not have a vision of their permanence on the planet nor the cooperation among themselves to reach a long term objective that few people understand.

Almost always, the conclusions reached at these Sunday gatherings were neither final nor clear, but debate was intense and generally well founded. Debate was always popular, and Toño's contribution was especially appreciated since he always had something of substance to say. The participation of young people was a surprise. It was always believed that the new generations did not have any interest in politics or economics, so it was amazing to see their participation during the debates. On occasion, when the supposed plastic recycling program was discussed, young people took over the topic and clearly demonstrated the tricks used by suppliers and producers. Toño tried not to miss any of the debates and the informal gatherings that followed. Despite his many occupations, he always made room for these sessions. In a certain way, it was the final glimmer of the unbreakable bond that had brought them all to the city. As long as the young people kept in touch with the original family line, and remembered the smell of the countryside, that connection would last and would feel authentic, as part of a whole which would never be separated. Sometimes, he liked to bring Rachel to the gatherings; he enjoyed her immersion in the discussions and her display of intelligence and knowledge. Toño's family had become used to her, either beside him or not, and she was never considered a stranger. It was as if she had always been a part of the family.

One day the discussion was centered around the topic of those leaving the country to never return. Toño insisted that once born into the Mexican culture you could never lose it, since it was a complete and existential life's vision. It was also argued, however, that even though Mexican culture that identifies you as a member of a community cannot be lost when acquired originally, in the case of all those Mexicans who have incorporated universal values from other cultures it is probably not a good experience when they return to Mexico, now a culture offering an incomplete vision of the world. For example, someone who adopts respect for human rights in a country where they are respected cannot accept its everyday abuse as it occurs in Mexico. This means that even though one's Mexican culture is never lost, when returning to Mexico from abroad, once universal values have been adopted, it is not possible to pretend to be truly Mexican in most cases. This forced us to ask what is the situation of those who have spent many years studying abroad? And those who left the country because of political conflicts and have not returned? And even more, all those who are out of the country?

Each has found an answer appropriate to their individual situation. Nevertheless, regardless of their own situation, when universal values from other cultures are added to one's personality the result is a belief system more humane, compassionate and less Mexican. Of course, the new generations of Mexicans will have the last word, for on them will depend the ultimate cultural shape that will make Mexican culture more universal and perhaps more humane.

In the end, Toño would say, "that those farmers who came to the city without hate and unarmed, will try to transform the State into the form necessary to attain development and viability. This time they would come showing compassion, generosity and kindness and they would not come exclusively from the North, but would come from every part of the country, even from abroad."

IV

"We got the chahuistle!"
Popular saying.

For Toño, the happiest period and the one with the greatest achievements was the time spent studying. He did it while working at all kinds of jobs and several different occupations. He was always glad to go to the classroom and discover the truths and secrets hidden in books by authors, mostly dead, during the sessions led by his professors; some, who had just recently been introduced to the topic they were teaching. It was fascinating to learn about the great effort made by humanity to spread knowledge: how Plato had learned from his teacher Socrates when knowledge was still passed on orally, and how great controversies then arose around writing and its influence on the human brain, similar to the debate regarding the introduction of computers, with their prodigious memory and their effects on human intellect and general learning today.

All these memories force him to consider his education and the Mexican system that had provided it. It had taken a huge effort, but the opportunity had been there, and he had taken advantage of it. When he first began his studies, there was a school in his town but unless your parents forced you to go to school there was no general understanding that an education was necessary to attain a better life. Once in the city, however, it became almost a religion to go to school, no one of a certain age could avoid it. At first it was compulsory by law, and then it became compulsory by decree of the community. Everybody, even women and the poorest of the poor, should go to school to learn, among other things, how to read and write. After elementary school it was optional to continue. Those with the ability to learn and those forced by their parents would continue to secondary school. From then on everyone was on his or her own. Some, like Toño, fell in love with knowledge and would stay in the classroom, others would continue in their family's business, but most left school and joined the thousands of workers in unskilled jobs or the many millions of unemployed.

Then came the moment when we all faced a sober reality. In the seventies it was said that 700,000 jobs were needed, taking into account the population

14

growth, to satisfy the needs of those looking for work. But the economy was never able to meet the demand, not even close to it; on the contrary, unemployment increased astronomically, as did illegal employment and the forced departure of nationals abroad, mostly to the United States of America. It was then when we all asked, "why do we have not only corrupt but also inept politicians?"

Toño was in the best place to answer this question, and soon gave a satisfactory explanation: "Mexican politicians, at least until the year 2000, stole large sums of money without having to worry about their responsibility to the country. This was only possible because they were part of an authoritarian pyramid that only had to fear their immediate superior and the President of the country. Consequently, full responsibility for the social and economic disasters of Mexico fell on the Presidents, who would take the politicians to the edge of the cliff from where, following his example, all would jump. The President of the country was the sole person accountable for the political and economic decisions made during at least 60 years (from 1940 to the year 2000) of Mexican history because that was the direction that had been taken at the end of the Mexican revolution."

"Why did the system continue to be structured in such a way? It was because the national Presidents had preferred not to modify a single aspect of the system after it was initially created. Lázaro Cárdenas completed the system in 1938 and, although Cárdenas wanted to establish a worker's democracy, the party ended up as a collection of political corporations where all the then important groups were represented (with the exception of the military), giving absolute power to the President. When Manuel Avila Camacho took over the presidency in 1941, he certainly did nothing to change the system, even though he has been credited for changing the name of the political party from PRM (Partido de la Revolución Mexicana) to PRI (Partido Revolucionario Institucional). All the subsequent Presidents kept the system and made it permanent, emphasizing the candidates' skill in the courtiers game, but who were generally inept with regard to the realities of governing a country. Some pretended to be great statesmen, such as Luis Echeverría and Carlos Salinas de Gortari, under whose administration the national economy and politics sadly suffered disastrous downfalls." Toño knew all this and he explained it to the young people during the opportunity afforded him at the Sunday gatherings.

There was a time when constitutional law fascinated Toño. It was the perfect combination of Law and Politics. He still vividly recalled the impressive

15

lectures of one of the law school scholars, who had referred to the significant principles inserted in the Apatzingan constitution of 1814 and then transferred to subsequent constitutions until becoming a part of the current 1917 constitution. It was a masterful presentation of the history of Mexico. Those principles, however, did not seem to be part of the society in which Toño lived.

Among these great principles were those that directly related to the law: that the law should be applied to everyone equally, and that life must be respected under any and all circumstances. These were great principles that unfortunately could not be applied in a place like Mexico. In Mexico, the law could not be equal for all since not all citizens were considered equal, some citizens being more important than others, and we as Mexicans could not miss at recognizing this reality. For example, even within a family the head of the family, the one who has reached the highest social status, is more important socially than everyone else, more so than his servants. And this way of thinking permeates all kinds of social relations. If that reasoning were not enough, there is the example of the great man of letters and scholar in charge of the constitutional lectures Toño attended: when one of the professor's favored students, someone who seldom attended class, had the nerve to recite the only topic he knew during an oral examination, the professor, having asked something totally different, protected him and allowed him to continue with a faultless record by ignoring his failure. It was then that Toño discovered that the great principles, in a country like Mexico, are more to be appreciated than to be applied. "Reality is different here", he used to say.

In spite of it all, Toño was genuinely happy living in a reality that sometimes might not exist. Those great principles had come from somewhere, and were applied somewhere to a certain population, and that excited him. It did not matter that those principles did not apply to his people. "Perhaps in the future they will," he said to himself.

Toño followed his destiny eagerly and with optimism. The explanation of the great past failures of the regime were more historical than contemporary. It fell upon him to explain that the government of today was not the government of the past. A new generation had taken control and it was not linked to the past. The Mexico of today did not live simultaneously in both the present and the past. Human sacrifices and authoritarianism had existed before, but did not exist now.

V

"If a pot is left boiling for a long time, the flavor is lost"
Popular saying.

At the Sunday gatherings people would frequently insist: Why were all the Presidents selected by the PRI given sole responsibility for the many economic crises of Mexico?

Toño said, "the answer is in fact quite simple. With great power, like the power vested in the Presidents selected by the PRI, comes great responsibility. None, with the exception perhaps of Lazaro Cardenas, were at the level of this responsibility. Mexico needed real statesmen and sadly they were conspicuous by their absence."

"When the Mexican revolution was over, the accepted ideology was the one proposed by the victors: Venustiano Carranza, a state governor, and Alvaro Obregon, a small businessman, neither of whom came from regions which could contribute to the acceptance of a non-capitalist ideology or to being away from the influence of the United States of America. After the murder of Venustiano Carranza, Alvaro Obregón and his successor Plutarco Elias Calles focused on the creation of a State based on threats of violence and warlordism. Their first important political action was the attempted destruction of the principle of "no reelection," that was not violated due to the assassination of President Obregon which left Calles as the only succesor. Calles subsequently controlled several Presidents, until he was retired by Lazaro Cardenas, who founded the Mexican Revolution Party (PRM) which with a new name (Partido Revolucionario Institucional, PRI.) would monopolize the future of politics in Mexico."

"At its foundation, in 1938, the PRI gathered all the important forces (with the exception of the military, as previously indicated), thus granting the president supremacy as the final decision maker in the political hierarchy of the country. As a result, the President became the commander in chief with the power to make final decisions, especially regarding all political and economic matters. At no time was that power disputed. True, some, at least initially, would suggest other options and others were even critical of the President's position, but at no time did the yes-men surrounding the President

17

allow anyone to raise their voice to suppress anything the President had to say."

"The clarity and certainty of the President's voice had many channels of dissemination that easily silenced any message from the opposition. All broadcast media was controlled by the presidential office and television, radio and the newspapers all existed and functioned thanks to the presidency. Their permits depended on the attention they gave to the propaganda and news from the government. The written press, in particular, owed its existence to the governmental control of their presses through distribution of paper. It was not uncommon for journalists who wrote favorable opinions or commentaries about the government or who avoided publishing real facts harming the regime, to receive juicy bribes. It was especially lucrative for most journalists to follow what the President and his inner circle said or did."

"The presidency was for all practical purposes, a revered institution, since what was said or done by the President was the law which everyone should obey. If the President especially appreciated the services of a particular politician, that person's rating would increase automatically. With regards to economic matters, the orders given by the President were not a matter for discussion, regardless of their real value. The power of the President was such, for example, that when the President's wife was denied a certain table in a popular restaurant, her bodyguards came back a few moments later and spread the place with machine gun fire with the disastrous result of a foreign tourist being shot. This unfortunate traveler happened to be vacationing in the wrong place at the wrong time. The recognition by foreign authorities of such events took several years, and the newspaper report never appeared in the local press "

"In Mexico exceptional people, and Presidents certainly fall into this category, feel that they belong to a special group that is considered by others as being infallible and subject to impunity. The embarrassments suffered by the Presidents starting with Díaz Ordaz, diminished the status of the presidential office. Although its importance was revived for a couple of years during the presidency of Carlos Salinas de Gortari, it never shone as before due to the Mexican public's awareness of its undeniable culpability for the economic crisis the country was still suffering."

"But the responsibility acquired by Mexican Presidents after the revolution can only begin to be conceived by explaining the absolute power that they all exercised." Toño continued. "The true magnitude of their lack of economic knowledge can be appreciated by their reactions to world circumstances present at the end of the Second World War, as well as to their lack of reaction when the gold-standard was abandoned by the government of the United States of America."

"During the period from 1940 to 1960, the world economy greatly favored Mexico: it was the golden period of capitalism when most capitalist countries prospered, to the extent that some countries took advantage of this international juncture to reach the status of advanced economies. But not Mexico. Politicians in power were satisfied with staying in power and fostering a growing economy that they said was as thriving and positive as their published statistics were showing."

"Managing the economy, even in the twenties, was not a matter for aficionados of economics, such as the Mexican Presidents. It was a serious control of a complex system. In 1920, after a brief period of expansion, the Mexican economy entered a period of recession, mainly due to the recession in the United States of America in 1927, which lingered until the American stock exchange fell in 1929 with the ensuing great depression."

"The great depression of the United States of America initially hit the Mexican economy hard. It had a multi pronged effect by reducing the demand for and prices of export goods, and as a consequence, decreasing the country's international reserves and taxable income. The factors which allowed Mexico to overcome these economic stumbling blocks was the increase in silver and other mining exports, as well as oil exports. Even more important, however, was the implementation of expansionist tax, monetary and exchange policies under the direction of economic advisor Alberto J. Pani in 1932. Soon silver and oil again became the main exports which allowed Mexico to receive an external incentive consisting of valuable imports, causing the economy to grow and thus allowing the import substitution needed."

"It was during the period of Lazaro Cardenas (1934-1940) that the state finally acquired all the modern tools to make possible a more active economic policy in order to face adverse conditions and even to stimulate the economy through budget deficits resulting in small deficits in the balance of payments. During the Second World War, for which the United States had been preparing since 1941, Mexico took the position that the economy must be protected, and that the development of industry should continue with import substitution and the creation of the needed infrastructure. The impact of the Second World War on Mexico, however, was felt in the flotation of the national currency in 1948-1949 and soon after in the resulting devaluation."

"In spite of missing the great opportunity of a favorable outcome during the Second World War, the entry of the United States of America in the Korean War in 1953 gave the Presidents of Mexico and their advisors a second opportunity to take a more informed approach. During the period of 1950 to 1962 the monetary, tax and credit policies were concerned mostly with external economic shocks, the devaluation of 1954, and the promotion of industry duly protected by the political structure. Despite everything, the impact of the external factors of the Korean War on the balance of payments was such that the currency had to be devalued from $8.65 to $12.50 under the direction of Antonio Carrillo Flores, this time as a preventive measure and with good results. Due to the favorable conditions of world capitalism and the weakening of the protectionist plan of the national industry, this period resulted in what is considered to be the best domestic growth rate ever experienced in Mexico. The Gross Domestic Product (GDP) grew 5.4% from 1950 to 1953, 8.2% from 1954 to 1957 and 5.2% from 1958 to 1962."

	GDP %	GDP millions Dollars			GDP %	GDP millions Dollars			GDP %	GDP millions Dollars	
	a	b	c		a	b	c		a	b	c
1940	1.31	1,528		1965	6.15	21,694	21.84	1990	5.21	228,424	262.7
1945	3.23	4,240		1970	6.50	35,542	35.52	1995	-6.29	302,547	360.1
1950	9.72	4,874		1975	5.74	88,008	88.00	2000	4.94	699,444	707.9
1955	8.48	7,204		1980	9.23	188,737	194.3	2005	2.31	892,871	877.5
1960	8.11	12,776	13.04	1985	1.88	102,661	184.5	2010	5.12	1,079,675	1,058.0

Sources: Data elaborated by the author from different sources, mostly amexicomaxico.org, Base 2013 in Termómetro de la economía mexicana, indicadores históricos 1935-2020. bInstituto Nacional de Estadística, Geografía e Informática (INEGI), Censos de Población y Vivienda. Tabulados encuesta intercensal 2009, 2011, 2015, 2016. cWorld Bank. IBRD, IDA, Data, México GDP, Data GDP.

Note: Economic statistics from the Mexican government are not reliable since most main series, especially those from the period 1940-1980 show some important inconsistencies, besides other relevant mistakes. For a simple example see note on pages 138-139 of the book El Pulso de los Sexenios by Miguel Basañez, as it applies to the population growth or notes in the article of Lustig and Székely, México: Evolución Económica: Pobreza y Desigualdad about data shown in their Appendices, pp.20-26.

"From 1963 to 1971 the GDP grew spectacularly by 7.1% and inflation was under control at 2.8%. Unfortunately that was the time when foreign credit started to flow, increasing the external debt of the country. But even more important, it was during this period when major decisions should have been made but were not. It was evident by now that there were four major problems: income distribution, a needed tax reform, the abandonment of agriculture and protest movements. During this period it also became clear that income and government social services were concentrated in a little over 20% of the country's population, (made up of political corporations such as the national Mexican oil workers union, for example) even though they insisted that the government statistics reflected the entire population of Mexican society."

Top 20% Share of Income

1950	1963	1968	1975	1977	1989	1992	1994	1998	2000	2005	2010	2016
54.9[a]	59.5[b]	58.4[b]	60.4[b]	53.7[b]	54.9[c]	56.6[c]	57.5[c]	57.3[d]	57.6[d]	55.2[e]	52.9[e]	54.2[e]
59.3[f]	58.0[f]	58.1[f]	62.1[f]	55.0[f]	59.2[e]	58.7[e]	59.0[e]	57.8[e]	57.6[e]	52.4[g]	50.1[f]	

Sources: Table elaborated by the author from several sources, [a]O. Altimir in Distribución del Ingreso en México 1950-1977. Ensayos (Banxico) Tomo I (1982) Cuadro 1, pp. 69. [b]O. Altimir in Distribución del Ingreso en México Ensayos (Banxico), O. Gomez & E. Arnaud, La Política Presupuestaria del Sector Público y su Incidencia en la Distribución del Ingreso, Tomo III Cuadro 4, p. 49. [c]F. Cortés, Distribución del Ingreso en México en Epocas de Estabilización y Reforma Económica, Charts 4 & 5 pp. 47 & 51. [d]F. Cortés, Medio Siglo de Desigualdad en el Ingreso de México, UNAM, Chart 1 & 3. [e]Index Mundi, Mexico Income Distribution, Chart, Income share held by highest 20%. [f]S. Sandoval Olascoaga The Distribution of Top Income in México. How rich are the richest? Appendix 3. [g]Instituto Nacional de Estadística, Geografía e Informática (INEGI), ENIGH, Distribution of Income.

Note: Sample income scores have been taken from many representative studies dealing with this subject showing a variable of income for the different decile sectors of the Mexican population. However, in no case these 20% top percentages (or IX and X deciles of the Mexican population) available exceed the 50.15 minimum and 62.14 maximum range. The average of the series shown is 59.19 and their median is 57.60.

VI

"The one who can, gives orders, the one who wants to, obeys them"
Popular saying.

"In fact, the great country of Mexico, according to the PRI, showed unusual progress in many important areas during its governance: population growth statistics were impressive, going from a rate of 1.73 in 1940 to 3.5 in 1960, childbirth mortality was greatly reduced from 126 deaths per thousand in 1940 to only 74.2 in 1960, illiteracy went from 47.88% of the population in 1940 to 30.22% in 1960, and even more remarkable, the GDP (in 1970 pesos per inhabitant) went from 3.56 to 6.44 thousand pesos in 1960, reflecting an annual per capita income of 2.76 thousand pesos in 1940 and 5.65 thousand pesos in 1960."

"Governments that came from the PRI have indicated that the so-called "Mexican miracle," the economic progress experienced during the period beginning in 1940 and continuing through 1982, had a very positive impact on the development of the country. Unfortunately this statement is only partially true. This period did not benefit the Mexican population as a whole, but it was especially advantageous for a specific group within the population who ended up enjoying greater economic growth and for far longer than in other countries. Ultimately income and privileges were concentrated in a small urban minority which, as stated before, motivated the Mexican farmers to decide to come to the cities."

	Mexico Total Population (Millions)			Mexico Rural Population	
				(Millions)	(%)
	Historical[a]	World Bank[b]		d	f
1940	19.6			15.30	78.11
1945	22.7			16.97	74.80
1950	26.2			18.61	71.06
1955	30.9			20.35	65.88
1960		37.7		22.87	60.68
1965		44.1		24.61	55.82
1970		51.4		26.21	51.01
1975		59.6		26.85	45.06

1980		67.7		26.84	39.66
1985		75.9		26.22	34.55
1990		83.9		24.06	28.68
1995		91.6		24.15	26.36
2000		98.8		24.98	25.29
2005		106.0		25.10	23.68
2010		114.0		25.30	22.20
2015		121.8		25.23	20.72

Sources: Table constructed with data from different sources, mostly: [a]Several historical statistic sources including Este País. Tendencias y Opinión, junio 2020, Chart I. Indicadores Demográficos de México de 1950 a 2050, Conapo, Gobierno de Mexico. Evolución de la Población de México 1900-2000. [b]World Bank, IBRD, IDA. Data, 2019. [d]Autor's calculations based on historical and World Bank data. [f]Rural percentage of total population.

"To achieve this the federal government had available thousands of millions of pesos to use as it pleased, and how it was distributed was decided by the President in office[4]. According to their own statistics[5], the government spent a total of $6,233,815 million pesos from 1940 to 1992 and averaged $1,755,045.61 million every year from 1993 to 2000, (all in current pesos) for a grand total of 20,274,179.88 million. Despite the economic success proclaimed by the government during the period from 1940 to 2000, its spending was concentrated on supporting industry, while expenditures assigned to directly benefit the population were negligible, in spite of government propaganda. The so-called indirect benefit was concentrated on the construction of infrastructure and the excessively burdensome payments to the bureaucracy. It was not until the seventies that spending planning was carried out more systematically, with the creation of the Ministry of Budget and Programing. However, it soon came into conflict with the Ministry of Finance."

"After 1960, Mexican Presidents decided that considering the success previously achieved (from 1940 to 1960) the same economic policy of 'stabilizing development' and substitution of imports should be followed; this time, however, in view of the changing external conditions and the lack of internal savings, financing would mostly be coming from abroad. Favorable statistics, now including the wave of farmers already in the cities, continued to

---

[4] See Impact of Governance Structure on Economic and Social Performance, by Joyce Ming, University of Pennsylvania, Scholarly Commons, 2008, p.35.

[5] Estadísticas Históricas de México, Tomo I, INEGI, Finanzas Públicas, pp. 629-630, Charts 17.3.1, 17.3.2.

increase. Nevertheless, the looming economic disaster moved closer. The rate of newborn deaths continued to drop until it reached 33.03 deaths per thousand in 1982, illiteracy rate was reported to be just a little more than 17% of the population that same year, and GDP, according to government data, was 12.36 thousand pesos (in 1970 pesos)."

	1940	1945	1950	1955	1960	1965	1970
Birth death rate per thousand	125.7	107.9	96.2	83.3	74.2	60.7	63.7
Life expectancy (years, men)	41.5	48.9	50.6	55.0	60.0	62.1	64.0
Illiteracy %	53.9		43.4		34.6		25.1

	1975	1980	1985	1990	1995	2000	2005	2010	2015
Birth death rate per thousand	49.0	37.2	28.8	24.4	17.6	14.2	10.5	10.1	10.0
Life expectancy (years, men)	66.8	70.0	71.8	75.0	75.7	76.4	76.6	77.0	77.4
Illiteracy %		17.8		12.2	8.9		6.9	5.5	

Source: Based on Instituto Nacional de Estadística, Geografía e Informática (INEGI), statistics.

VII

"Chuchita was robbed!"
Popular saying.

"By 1982 Mexico had experienced at least two other earlier great crises: one almost unseen in 1968 and another a much more evident one in 1976. The 1968 crisis was political and had to do mostly with the legitimacy of the government, which triggered the appearance of guerrilla groups in Mexico and was the beginning of the end of political support that the government had previously enjoyed from the middle class. The 1976 crisis was both political and economic and resulted in the devaluation of the peso and the disrepute of President Echeverría."

This time the pending questions did not allow Toño to sleep, as he was afraid his answers would trap him not allowing him to defend his job but forcing him instead to attack the actions of the government. He did not believe that those who worked in public service should be held responsible for the personal misfortune of so many needy persons. Nevertheless, everytime an image of those forgotten souls, in dirty rags and without hope occupied his mind, his spirit would fill with hatred and contempt for the privileged, like himself, with whom he interacted everyday.

Toño did not pay much attention to domestic chores. Washing dishes and cooking did not seem appropriate tasks for someone destined to be important, and yet he still had to wash some of his clothes, those most often used, and he would ponder while doing it, that far from being humiliating, helped him remember his humble origins and made him aware of reality. He knew well that he had been born to reflect and to criticize. His rebellious nature made him feel comfortable with his tirades and it was not only a matter of undoing wrongs, but of also looking for the truth wherever it might be found. It was because of that trait that he had many enemies. Anyone who refused to discover the truth would suffer his resolve and forthrightness.

But if daily chores annoyed him, both study and work excited him. He was so immersed in these that it was customary to see him arrive home very late after a full day of work and study. No one could keep up with his pace nor carry out all his orders. He soon filled his room with books from wall to wall and dedicated himself to the study of the social sciences, especially as they applied to Mexico.

His first formal job, after working on and off in the upholstery shop, was in a bank, one of many banks throughout the city. His educational preparation and his skill with numbers were two factors that allowed him to advance and prosper in that institution. Before long, however, the activities became boring and predictable and it was clear that he had reached the limit to his advancement, unless he considered forming part of the family owning the banking operation. Although he contemplated such an option, there were many opportunities in a relatively young country like Mexico, especially in the public sector, where an educated and skillful person is more than welcome. As a matter of fact, employment within the government was something he had always wanted. It was the end of the nineties, he was 27 years old, and the promise of a new world was available to his generation.

When Toño started working in the government, the Cardenas era had ended a long time ago and the question of how to govern was becoming complicated. It was especially difficult to determine which economic policy to follow. On the one hand, national industrial production was promoted and an effort was being made to open the border to exports; on the other, imports were admitted into the country if sponsored by a politician or an important tycoon. Obviously, industrial development was very important, however, that policy started to harm rural agricultural production due to decreasing subsidies. At the beginning of the sixties the continued growth of the economy could not be supported with domestic savings alone; foreign credit was needed. This became obvious by the year 2000, although it was not as clear during earlier periods, unless you were familiar with basic macroeconomic concepts, as were the economic advisors to the government.

The debate topic of that week was still on the reasons why those Presidents identified with the PRI should be repudiated by every Mexican.

During the Sunday gathering, Toño focused on the period from 1940, when the PRI was fully formed, until 1994, when Carlos Salinas de Gortari and Ernesto Zedillo destroyed the country's economy for the third time (the first time it was ruined by Luis Echeverría in 1976, and the second time by José López Portillo in 1982). Government statistics and their interpretation indicated that the regime was doing very well, but this was not true. The period from 1960 to 2000, according to the government, enjoyed even greater success, although it was achieved with borrowed funds and in a totally different world economic environment, in which the gold-standard had been abandoned and inflation was the main enemy of capitalist countries, this without taking into account the rising interest rate of foreign debt for debtor countries like Mexico.

Reluctantly, Toño shared the history of the national economic crises. "In the sixties the policy of substituting imports created a non-competitive international industrial sector, and the then current President, Gustavo Diaz Ordaz, adopted a populist doctrine and the concept of a welfare state, and furthermore, concluded that the national economy needed an expansionist stimulus. It therefore became necessary to modify the economic policy of the group in power, increasing the social expenditures of the government. Unfortunately, domestic savings were not sufficient to cover these new investments, and funds were secured from abroad. When Luis Echeverría became President, he tried to modify the economic policy by offering the so-called 'shared development' continuing the substitution of imports but adding a pretended redistribution of income. Regrettably, the accumulation of errors, both political and economic, had damaged the presidency, and the exchange rate with the peso eventually had to be devalued in 1976."

"According to the Mexican government, things could have not been better in 1977: the country floated in oil, which guaranteed wealth for everyone; the private sector, reluctant initially, joined the general enthusiasm of the United States of America's banking sector that had granted major lines of credit to the company Alfa, a leader in the Mexican private sector, as well as to other public and private companies. Mexico almost instantaneously became a rich country which most world banks besieged. The economic disruption that followed was the result of incredible ineptitude, in which the government played an important role, and in which the resulting distrust and intense flight of foreign capital could not be avoided. The government could neither prevent the devaluation from 27.06 to 47.27 pesos for each United States of America dollar toward the end of 1982, nor the increased cost of tortillas, bread and gasoline for the ordinary citizen. Inflation, that is the fall in money's real value, was 4.69% in 1970, 29.85% in 1980, 63.75% in 1985 and 51.97%[6] in 1995. Foreign debt, measured as a percentage of GDP, jumped from 2.8% to 4.63% in 1960, and then would increase to 17.05% in 1970, 31.41% in

---

[6] Inflation.eu Worldwide Inflation Data. In terms of U.S. dollars. For a better understanding of these events see Enrique Cárdenas, Leopoldo Solís, David Ibarra, Carlos Tello & José López Portillo.

1980 and 56.8%[7] in 1994. The final blow to this economic tragedy was the nationalization of the banking system and the generalized control of currency exchange (which went to a fixed dual exchange rate of 50 and 70 pesos per United States of America dollar) by the regime."

[7] countryeconomy.com Mexico National debt. For figures referring to debt servicing see Enrique Cárdenas. La Política Económica en México 1950-1994, Table V. 5. p. 216, as well as the website of mexicomaxico.org

VIII

"Raining on soil already wet"
    Popular saying.

"When Miguel de la Madrid became President in 1983, his agenda clearly favored the foreign institutions and banks of the United States of America, not the people of Mexico, who were still, like today, immersed in poverty. It was at this time that those Presidents with economic studies in the United States, the so-called 'technocrats,' initiated a remarkable economic change in the country. First, Mexico entered the Generalized System of Commerce and Tariffs (GATT), and a few years later, started negotiations with the United States of America and Canada to agree on a Free Trade Treaty (NAFTA). Under Miguel de la Madrid two fundamental changes were initiated: a reduction in the size of the public sector and the opening up of the economy to the competition abroad."

"The great change would be completed by President Carlos Salinas de Gortari, who, worried about having assumed the Presidency by a supposedly fraudulent election, took measures to ensure his own personal legitimacy and to establish in México the neoliberal principles adopted by the Washington Consensus. Mexican society would now be regulated by these principles, which highlighted the stability, deregulation, privatization and opening up the economy."

"The Washington consensus is considered one of the clearest expressions of neoliberalism, an economic doctrine that in Mexico included several requirements. The first requirement was to stabilize the economy by addressing the need to reduce the rate of inflation. In Mexico this was implemented under the program known as the 'Pact of Economic Solidarity,' starting in 1987 and lasting until 1989, that consisted in opening the Mexican market to foreign competition in certain industries. The second requirement of the consensus, when Mexico joined the GATT in 1987 and began full negotiations to establish a trade treaty with the United States of America and Canada, was to open the economy. After having been a totally closed economy, Mexico became one of the countries with the most international trade treaties. In 1986 and 1987 the country suffered the consequences of the anti-inflationary policy and the opening of the markets when several industries disappeared or were decimated. The third requirement was deregulation, that in Mexico meant to modify applicable regulations by making them less restrictive, to modify the 'ejido' ground rules, and to diminish the public presence of the Church. Finally, the fourth requirement was the privatization of the economy that started in 1991, which meant that many companies, including the nationalized banks, went back to the private sector."

"In 1994, after what seemed like a great recovery, both the economy and politics fell at the same time: foreign capitals left the country and commercial debt interest increased considerably; subcomandante Marcos and his guerilla fighters appeared in Chiapas and, sometime later, Donaldo Colosio, a presidential candidate, and Jose Francisco Ruiz Massieu, General Secretary of the PRI, were assassinated. The peso was devalued again and President Clinton, of the United States of America, had to arrange a financial rescue package involving several international organizations. Mexico, on its own, created the Bank Fund to Protect Savings (Fobaproa), in a desperate attempt to save its financial system."

"Fobaproa was created by the Bank of Mexico to finance the banking sector and thus avert the failure of the financial system. It was done by requiring that existing credits in default by bank clients and considered bad bank debts be documented with government obligations, payable in ten years at an interest higher than Treasury Certificates of Mexico (CETES). The banks maliciously included dubiously qualified debt in the fund, and the government prevented the identification of these debts by giving CETES bearing regular interest in exchange. This fund exceeded 800 thousand million pesos."

"In spite of it all," Toño added, "the country once again recovered. On this occasion it was mainly due to the exportation of manufactured products, in good part from the in-bond industries established by United States of America companies in Mexican states located mostly along the northern border of the country."

"Some permanent economic trends were, however, established for the future: between 1980 and 2010 total merchandise exports rose from 39.1 billion to 599.8 billion with oil exports decreasing to only 17.4% of total exports in

2008. 'Although Mexico trade[d] around the world and absorbe[d] investment from many countries, the United States is its most important partner.'[8] This partnership was consolidated in 2010, with total of 79.9% of Mexican merchandise exports going to the United States, mostly as part of production-sharing agreements. The three main manufacturing groups consistently imported and exported between Mexico and the United States of America have been electrical machinery and equipment, non-electrical machinery and motor vehicles and parts."

[8] United States and Mexico: Ties that Bind, Issues that Divide. RAND Corporation, p. 95

IX

"Do not give me anything, but put me where there is some"
Popular saying.

"But why do you say that every Mexican must repudiate those Presidents selected by the PRI? After all, they were placed in the position of 'kings' of the country and, like existing monarchies, they cannot be guilty of much," someone asked.

"True, monarchies still exist but they are mere symbols of their countries and whether they deserve to exist or not, they do participate in almost none of the important decisions in their societies. The case of Mexico is different. The 'kings' named by the Mexican political system are not merely symbolic, they decide on and execute all functions of a modern state, in particular those economic activities that affect society as a whole. When appointed, they inherit the great responsibility of improving the living conditions of the Mexican people and to use the country's resources wisely," answered Toño.

"Furthermore, the Mexican government, from the start, was not transparent. It secretly used the country's resources without sharing much information on how it handled them. The scarce information made public during this period (from 1940 to 1982) mostly favored the government. Then, guessing a little and as it has been established by the experts, it is known that the presidential illiteracy campaigns were not successful.[9] Although education at that time received a supposedly high percentage of the of the government expenditures, the truth is that it was a relatively low amount compared to other countries (for example, in 2018 on average all countries in the Organization for Economic Co-operation and Development [OECD] allocated 20.1% of their Gross Domestic Product [GDP] for social expenditures, or $12,085,543.44 million US dollars, while Mexico only

---

[9] Ver Journal AED Adult Education Development 71/2008 por Carmen Campero, Luz Ma. Castro y Carmen Diaz. También, Analfabetismo en Mexico: Una deuda social por Jose Narro Robles y David Moctezuma Navarro en Revista Internacional de Estadística y Geografía, Vol 3, septiembre-diciembre 2012

budgeted 7.5% or $193,466.19 million[10]). The same could be said of the health sector which in spite of the Mexican government's public self-congratulatory statements, received very small allocations from the country's budget . It was not until the sixties and seventies that the idea of the welfare state, which was started and established by developed countries, was finally partially adopted by the country. However, Mexico could never reach the level of implementation or the allocation percentages of these countries. The decision of the Mexican state to provide these benefits, despite the lack of resources, was probably one factor that helped do away with the moderate direction of the economic policy. Nevertheless, it did allow for, even if through the use of foreign credit, the establishment of pensions for privileged groups, expansion of housing construction, the increase in social expenditures and other economic data but only in favor of a small percentage of people. The first international report on social expenditure in Mexico given by the OECD in 1981, showed very low percentages when compared to other countries in the region."

"In education, the government provided funding for the creation of new schools and to pay for new teachers. However, due to the accelerated growth of the student population, especially in the cities, this expenditure by the Mexican government was insufficient to result in any great advancement. (The OECD reported data of social expenditure in education by the Mexican government during the period of 1989 to 2016 to average a very low 4.26 of GDP). In fact, it is difficult to believe that the government had any concrete objectives to achieve, other than to provide space for an increasing school-age population. From 1958 to 1970 Mexico's population grew from 35.4 to 51.4 million inhabitants. Conversely, the average government expenditure for education in terms of GDP was less than 3.5%. It is estimated that in 1980, the population between 13 to 18 years of age had a 35% probability of entering high school, with only an 11% probability to enter higher education of those between 18 to 25 years of age. Nonetheless, this was a great improvement since in 1930 only 1% attended high school. Available statistics indicate that higher education attendance increased from 0.7% to 1.53% of the total of the population from 1951 to 1985, showing an average of only

[10] Data of Mexico's GDP given by the organization OECD indicates a figure for Mexico in 2018 of $2,579,549.2 U.S. dollars equivalent to a GDP of $23,543,546.0 in current millions of pesos calculated using ppp. (Average estimated OECD was $60,127,081.8 U.S. current dollars using ppp).

0.55% during the period from 1950 to 1987 (in most developed countries it was between 40 and 50%)."

Total expense in Education as percentage of GDP[a]

	1980	1985	1990	1993	1995	1998	2000	2010
Federal Expense	4.6	3.9	4.0	5.3	4.9	6.0	6.8	6.7
School System	3.5	3.0	3.0(2.3)[b]	4.3	4.2(3.6)[b]	4.1	4.1(3.9)[b]	--
Elementary	1.3	1.0	1.3	2.0	2.2	2.6	2.7	--
Senior High	0.3	0.3	0.3	0.4	0.5	0.4	0.4	--
College	0.6(1.35)[b]	0.5(1.53)[b]	0.5	0.7	0.8	0.8	0.7	--
Other	1.2	1.2	1.6	1.2	0.7	0.3	0.3	--
Private Expense	0.3	0.3	0.3	0.3	0.2	1.1	1.2	--

Source: [a]IMF, Corbacho & Gerd Schwartz, International Monetary Fund (IMF), Working Paper WP/02/12, pp. 20 and 21. [b]Miguel Basañez, El Pulso de los Sexenios, pp. 154 & 143.

"These and other results raise doubts about the achievements proclaimed by the government; there is little doubt that large amounts of money, according to the government, were assigned to education. However, to state this in terms of percentages of the national budget distort (and considerably increase) the totals that are normally given in percentages of GDP, which were still relatively low."

X

"Tree that is born bent, would never have its trunk straightened"
Popular saying.

"There is also doubt about the country's progress regarding public health[11], in spite of the amounts allocated to it, when compared with the amounts designated to it by other countries, even those in Latin America."

"Social Security in Mexico covered '4.3% of the population in 1950, 11.5% in 1960 and 25.3% in 1970,' which represented both a challenge and an opportunity for the government that unfortunately did not know how to or could not manage. Behind the declared progress, it was clear that the true intention of the Presidents was to use the insufficient country's investment funds on the privileged few rather than on the majority."[12]

"In Mexico from 1958 to 1970 the government expenditure allocated to health was less than 2% of GDP on average. However, one must not forget that the rural population was invading the cities, and that distorted the data on medical services. Furthermore, medical coverage was offered by both the public and the private sectors (but the government reports only referred to total expenditures of approximately 5% of GDP in 1995, 6.2% in 2012 and 5.6 in 2015, when in fact public expense was less than 3%). It will always be argued that during this period and under these Presidents, the country provided medical services to a large portion of the private population who in reality were paying the country's medical professionals directly (in fact, these patients were a little more than half of the population reported and they spent slightly little less than half of the total amount paid for health services); that newborn deaths continued to decrease, going from 126 deaths in 1940 to only 33 in 1982 and 13 today; and that the average life expectancy for men went from 35 years in 1940 to 75 years today. In truth, the amounts allocated by the government to health care were really low and the achievements of the government programs were believable, though clearly exaggerated since such

[11] In Tomoko Murai in The Developing Economies. Mexico. p. 266. Para datos similares ver Carmelo Meza-Lago Social Security, Stratification and Inequality in Mexico. pp. 238-240.
[12] See tables on Financing of the Economy and Sector contribution to the Economy in the Additional Statistical Appendix in this work, pp. 84 & 85.

achievements, such as an increase in the population's life expectancy, a reduction in the child' birth death rate and an increase in literacy, were the result of both government action and policy, as well as practical measures taken by the general public."

Health expenses, Percentage – Source & Origin[a] %

	1993	1994	1997	1998		1993	1994	1997	1998
Source					Origin				
Families	50.3	49.1	61.2	57.5	Social Security	42.4	42.6	32.2	32.8
Employers	29.1	28.3	17.8	18.4	w/o Insurance	12.8	12.9	11.5	11.3
Federal gov.	19.4	19.7	20.7	23.8	Private expense	42.4	41.9	56.3	23.9
State gov.	1.2	2.9	0.3	0.3	Private Insurance	2.4	2.6	0	0

Health expenses % GDP[b] National comparison Health expenses (% GDP)[cd]

	1996	1998	1999	2000
Public expense	2.3	2.6	2.6	2.5
Private expense	2.8	3.0	2.9	--
Total expense	5.1	5.5	5.5	--

	OECD	Japon	Canada	Chile	Mexico
1990	4.351	4.442	6.22	--	1.748
2000	4.868	5.829	5.741	3.332	2.196
2011	5.941	7.689	7.183	3.061	2.819
2012	5.953	7.72	7.172	3.225	2.995

Sources: [a]Profile of the Health Services System, Mexico, Pan American Health Organization (PAHO), 1998 & 2002, p. 13, Dirección General de Información y Evaluación del Desempeño y la Secretaría de Salud (DGIED/SSA) Cuenta de Salud Nacional. [b]Jose B Ramirez, El Colegio de la Frontera Norte 2012. Costos de los Servicios de Salud. [c]Data of World Inequality Database (WID). [d]OECD Social Expenditure, January, 2019.

"As for the presidential literacy campaigns, as it was previously mentioned, they clearly failed due to the fact that a change in the social structure was required, but it was not offered."

"However, an initiative of the government as well as civil society produced a popular culture that reduced the illiteracy rate among 15-29 year-olds, although the same cannot be said of the older population and of the indigenous groups that spoke other languages. Based on official sources, it is reported that 6.9% of the population or 7,751,221 people were illiterate in 2010, mostly in rural areas. (In 2019 the government reported 5.5% or

4,749,057 illiterate people in the country, but their calculations have traditionally been subject to manipulation[13])."

"It is also necessary to take into account that the government had started to lose its absolute control over society. After the 1985 earthquake that resulted in thousands of deaths and great destruction in Mexico City, citizens began to organize themselves and stopped depending on a political system that obviously could not respond to a major emergency and could not manage the economy correctly. The loss of control was evidenced also by the fact that the population of Mexico grew during the period under consideration at an uncontrollable annual rate, by 1.73% in 1940 to 3.14% in 1974, when it began to decrease. In other words, the population grew from 20 million in 1940 to 73 million in 1982, and to more than 120 million today. The rural population went from 78.1% in 1940 to only 32.5% in 1982, decreasing to 22% in 2010. Part of the truth is that the categories normally mentioned by the government as examples of a growing economy, refer to the consequences and are evidence of an uncontrollable growth of a population intent on becoming more urban than rural and more civil than political," explained Toño.

"It was the year 2000 when the Mexican government went to the conservatives for two six-year periods. Unfortunately, these administrations did not offer any programs that were any different than those offered by the PRI Presidents. Firstly, the President continued to be the figure that the revolution had created, though perhaps a little less authoritarian and with less control. Secondly, many of the new public officials considered their new positions as an opportunity to become wealthy. Thirdly, even though new institutions were established, like the popular health insurance, which in theory, insured the health of almost 40% of the total population without medical service, the new governments did not even pretend to modify much of what the previous regimes had established, especially as regards public security and corruption."

But Toño had neither the time nor the opportunity to defend the government, after referring to these data that, even though they raised considerable doubt about his government position, did not excuse the regime of such a huge disaster. As an expert on the difficulties and turns of public

[13] See Chart 2 and comments, Alfabetizados por el INEA in Revista Internacional de Estadística y Geografía, Vol 3, Number 3, September-December, 2012. Analfabetismo en Mexico: Una deuda Social by Jose Narro Robles & David Moctezuma Navarro.

organizations, he had a lot to say, and his justification for being a federal government bureaucrat was to remain in abeyance. "Do not miss next Sunday's gathering. I promised you that my statements will be worth your while. Societies are very complex organizations, and it is therefore not possible to place the blame on only one institution."

XI

"I am myself and I am like no one else…"
Popular song.

Still thinking about what he had said at the past Sunday gathering, Toño spent a week of reflection and self-justification. It was going to be necessary to show once and for all that managing the State is not a simple thing to do. Most good theories could not practically be applied immediately and the State could not afford to make a mistake. There was also the issue of the money that flowed among important public officials.

Upon returning to his job, Toño did not stop thinking about what was waiting for him next Sunday next week. It was, nothing less, than the moment to defend his personal position and to present a clear and final description of a government that had obviously failed. This is why he advanced his allegations and decided to discuss the core question – why did we believe that the State must benefit most of the population? – with his subordinates. Without dressing up his question, Toño asked only Ovidio for his reasons.

After all, what had happened in the past did not make him responsible in the present. On the other hand, what was being done today affected him directly now that he was a federal bureaucrat with full access to authority. Politicians representing the State should not steal and act ineptly since they received excellent salaries and all kinds of privileges granted to them by their political power. The public, and above all the employees of the State, had the obligation to ensure that stealing and incompetency did not happen.

His coworkers and government employees were quite different from him, some were people who belonged to a different social stratum. Someone had even boasted of having his own swimming pool, an unusual luxury among his friends. However, most of them, especially those with whom he worked closely, were respectable representatives of the bourgeoisie, and although from time to time they would complain about the social structure in which they lived, they were comfortable with the reality of their existence and the society they sometimes criticized.

You could say that Ovidio Solis was the ideal member of the group. A mature and educated man, he had a sharp mind and good memory. You could say he was bright; however, he still closely held the ethical principles that were surely imbued in him by his parents while he was still a child during his religious upbringing. The most prominent was surely Manuel Lazcano, recently arrived from abroad – Philadelphia in the United States of America – where he had studied a specialty in economics. Although somewhat unsure of himself, he had a tremendous grasp of economic variables and the construction and execution of algorithms, concepts that were absolutely necessary to know in the modern age. The most brilliant, without a doubt, was Rogelio Cruz, a young man who was the product of the public education system. Like Toño, he too had overcome all kinds of obstacles until becoming a very valuable advisor to any first-rate politician. His insight and intelligence singled him out as unique, and his knowledge and instinct put him in a special group.

They all were extremely loyal to Toño, but at the same time felt greatly attached to the government. They would acknowledge not only this connection to an institution, but also their loyalty, which was beyond what is normal to Toño; both of these would surely overcome the most difficult challenges. Without their knowing it, their attachment and loyalty would soon be tested.

"Ovidio, do you believe that a State must provide apart from protection, benefits and services to most people?" Toño asked.

"That is a question answered a long time ago in the affirmative. Governments, if they want to be relevant to the people, must provide education, entertainment, health benefits and what is known as public services as a minimum," he firmly answered.

"Do you believe that the Presidents selected by the PRI are responsible for the ancestral backwardness of our people? Do you think they are guilty?" Toño asked.

"Yes, I believe they should be held responsible for causing the backwardness of our society and the misery in which we live," said Ovidio without much reflection.

"Why do you say that, without even giving it a second thought? insisted Toño.

"Because it is clear that we would not be in this economic predicament but for their mistakes." Ovidio answered, with a sad face.

"But you have to admit that the country has advanced a lot since the revolution of 1910," affirmed Toño emphatically.

"I am talking about what the government that rose out of the revolution has done until now, which is not much," replied Ovidio with sarcasm.

"Do you believe that both economic and political crises are exclusively the fault of the Presidents?" asked Toño again.

"I believe, if you let me speak frankly, that all crises, political as well as economic, are the result of the decisions or lack of decisions made by *los señores* Presidentes, who could have averted the crisis or at least they could have made them less damaging." reflected Ovidio.

Ovidio's answers were not headed in the right direction, and Toño needed to know his real opinion, not the opinion of a bureaucrat trying to protect his job.

"Let's pick a concrete example. If you agree, let's look at Echeverría's presidency and his huge economic failure of ignoring the then recent modification of the fixed exchange rate introduced by the United States of America, and of also ignoring the inflationary pressure caused by the oil increase in oil prices by the Arab countries. Both events contributed to the devaluation of the Mexican peso in 1976 at the end of Echeverría's term. Echeverría also alienated Mexican and foreign businessmen with his populist and, to a certain degree, radical declarations. If it is fine with you," continued Toño, "Echeverria's decisions did make sense if you consider that he was trying to avoid a resurgence of a political problem similar to the one experienced in 1968."

"No, it doesn't make any sense, even when taking a strictly political viewpoint. If he had been considering this point of view, he should have found support among leftist forces and those businessmen supporting his policies, but it was not like that. The destabilization resulted to a good extent from actions taken by the United States of America and to the Mexican economic policy abroad," stated Ovidio.

"Would you say that external forces were determining factors in the destabilization of the country during the period from 1970 to 1976?" Toño ended up asking.

"I believe they played an important role, but the mistakes made by President Echeverría were fundamental in the destabilization during that period," stated Ovidio. "It is clear that Echeverría was a megalomaniac whose delusion of grandeur was evident in his personal actions, in his operation of the dirty war, in his involvement of the events of 1968, in his contempt of the

Mexican private sector, and finally, in his pretension to continue as President or to obtain another important position on an international level."

"Do you believe, then, that the country was in the hands of a megalomaniac who tried to reverse the principle of no reelection?" replied Toño.

"If it was not in the hands of a megalomaniac, it was in the hands of a very sick person," Ovidio agreed.

"However, Jose Lopez Portillo's term started on normal grounds, taking all the existing circumstances into account," said Toño.

"Sadly, that period not only ended badly but became one of the most tragic in the history of the country."

"I believe that the absolute power arising from the Mexican political system would negatively affect anyone, but more so those who have megalomaniac tendencies," finished Ovidio.

"Echeverría, nevertheless, took some measures in favor of those he governed, wore a guayabera, and expanded the public sector and its imports considerably," said Toño in his defense.

"Unfortunately, he did not have a good economic plan and his measures were useless. Loans received to support imports ended up subsidizing the flight of capital. What was paid for the construction of the steel mill Lazaro Cardenas and the nuclear plant Laguna Verde is still remembered. Also remembered is his suspension of the birth control program, among other programs, due to the lack of funds, as was claimed at that time. Perhaps he intended to benefit most people initially, but he ended up hurting everybody in the end," pointed out Ovidio.

"In your opinion, then, Echeverría did not care about the ordinary people, in spite of his dress and his talk?" asked Toño.

"In truth, no. His actions were always directed towards his own benefit, no one else's, including the Mexican people," answered Ovidio with emphasis.

Toño reflected deeply on what Ovidio had said and posed a final question:

"If you disapprove of what the government did back then, why do you continue working for the same master?" Toño asked dispassionately.

"In the first place, what happened is in the past. These events and Echeverría's megalomania happened many years ago" Ovidio said, intending to make a list.

"But its aftermath is still harming those working for the government," interrupted Toño.

"True, but today there is the hope that things are going to be different with the introduction of free elections, new political parties, and the emergence of civil society," Ovidio replied.

It is true that our job is justified by the hope that we will do it better, thought Toño, but that does not mean that we are doing it better or that we are free from blame. The creation of a monster like Mexico's presidency will always be a problem if it is not restrained somehow.

XII

"If I say that the mule is brown, it is because I have her hairs in my hand"
Popular saying.

It was appropriate to continue with interviews that were previously begun, now that it was clear that neither Echeverría nor any other President selected by the PRI was loved, perhaps with the exception of Lazaro Cardenas. Toño's next step was to meet with Manuel, insisting on his answering truthfully. Coming from abroad, he might have a different point of view. Toño was not sure whether that was an advantage or a disadvantage. In any case, he would ask Manuel for his honest opinion, without taking into account his personal situation.

"In your opinion, is there anything degrading about working for the Mexican government, taking into account its past history of economic crises?" asked Toño initially.

"If I believed that I wouldn't be here. I think it is a real challenge trying to solve the problems that we face and it would be an honor to be the person upon whom this responsibility falls," answered Manuel.

"Doesn't it bother you that previous governments, especially those selected by the PRI, have made huge economic and political mistakes, thereby harming most people? insisted Toño.

"It bothers me up to a certain point, but on the other hand those mistakes have allowed me to try to rectify the course and especially their consequences," said Manuel.

"Do you think that the Presidents selected by the PRI should be repudiated for their ineptitude and lack of responsibility toward the common people?" Toño asked directly.

"That is a question that is difficult for me to answer. I was not living in Mexico during the events caused by the Presidents concerned. But I think that to miss out on the special opportunity to raise Mexico to the level of many developed countries would be unforgivable," stated Manuel, adding "I personally do not repudiate them, but I understand how many Mexicans would feel that way now that the country is floundering because of them."

What Manuel said made sense and Toño felt it was genuine.

It was now Rogelio's turn; surely Rogelio had a definitive opinion in this regard.

"Do you think that the population of Mexico should repudiate the Presidents selected by the PRI due to their ineptitude and the political and economic crises they put the country through, without worrying about the people in general?" asked Toño right away.

"I believe the Presidents selected by the PRI were individuals who, at least initially, arose from the social revolution that impacted Mexico from 1910 to 1917. Subsequently, they were inheritors of that same revolution. Being good or bad was all the country had to offer then," said Rogelio.

"But surely, you can identify two distinct periods since the revolution: one conservative, cautious and responsible, until 1960, and the one risk-taking, loquacious and irresponsible, until the year 2000, when the PRI lost the presidency," said Toño clarifying.

"Again, I insist that regardless of their achievements or culpability, they are public figures that the revolution and its aftermath produced. Their guilt or lack of it has not much to do with the way they were. The revolution became a government that was characterized by loyalty, praise and threats of violence; nothing noble and intelligent can come from a system with these values, and the ascension to the top of dysfunctional individuals was only a matter of time," answer Rogelio wisely.

"Why, then, are you a federal bureaucrat if, like you say, the government was inefficient and corrupt, without any concern for the benefit of the majority of the people?" continued Toño.

"I am a bureaucrat because we are not talking about the same government, but even if we were, I would rebel from within if such were the case. I have always believed that you can only fix a government from the inside," he said, "and that was the fundamental situation at the time. Either you accepted the government and its behavior and corruption, or you did not participate in the government, without much hope of having any influence," Rogelio justified himself in emphatic terms.

"This means, then, that the public is justified in repudiating them for their mistakes and character," said Toño in conclusion.

"The Presidents are certainly despicable, not only for who they are, but for what they represent. All of them, from Miguel Alemán to Salinas de

Gortari, are cut from the same cloth when it comes to authoritarianism, political and economic ineptitude, corruption and unconcern for the majority of the people," stated Rogelio.

"Do you mean you wouldn't be ashamed of a behavior as deplorable as that of Lopez Portillo having to devalue the currency, wasting a historical chance for the country to be wealthy and ending up with an unpayable debt?" asked Toño, guessing that Rogelio was trying to justify the Presidents.

"Yes, it is shameful to support someone taking such actions, but no one had much opportunity or possibility to oppose them. Whatever the President said had to be done," said Rogelio, emphasizing these words.

"You would have not resigned, had you been a federal bureaucrat at that time?" asked Toño again.

"No, my job was all I had, and I could not have found another one like it. Besides, the nationalization of the banking industry was the correct response to the denationalization made by the private sector. Lopez Portillo did the right thing, even if, in the end, de la Madrid had to comply with the requirements demanded by the United States of America and the International Monetary Fund to get out of the quagmire," Rogelio declared.

"But you would agree that defending the free exchange rate of the peso was not the best decision," asked Toño again.

"Truly it was not, like it was not the best decision to immediately develop and sell recently discovered oil without having a development plan," added Rogelio. "Lopez Portillo never intended to benefit the entire population of the country, since he still held a dual view of the population: on the one hand, the middle and upper classes, living mainly in Mexico City and other large cities; on the other hand, the rest of the population, those mostly living in rural areas, and the poor living in the cities. For him, economic progress mostly belonged to the first group. In the end, he never fought for the poor, his fight was against the rich who could transfer large sums of money out of the country with no concern for the ultimate consequences. Lopez Portillo had many failures, and these contributed to the lack of credibility in the office of the President. But I repeat, the system created by the revolution transformed him into the almost fictional character that most people condemn today, and it therefore could have not been any different," Rogelio ended up saying.

"Your stand allows you, then, to answer yes and no at the same time. On the one hand, Mexicans should repudiate the Presidents selected by the PRI because of their ineptitude and for the economic and political crises they brought about without worrying about the majority of the people, but also in your view the political system created by the revolution formed the Presidents and gave them the necessary power to be able to commit such excesses. Consequently, the Presidents selected by the PRI should not be repudiated since they were, up to a certain point, victims of the system," said Toño in conclusion.

"I would not be as generous as to interpret your answer as an excuse to absolve the Presidents of Mexico, after 1940, of their institutional responsibility," Toño added, thinking about his answer.

"It is not an unconditional justification. The Presidents selected by the PRI are personally guilty, but their responsibility should be measured based on the understanding that they belonged to a group that traditionally forced them to act in a certain way," elaborated Rogelio.

"This way of thinking exonerates them without taking into account that they are all guilty, in some way or another. You exclude, for example, the state murders or the presidential bribes. You are guilty from the moment you accept your first mission or your first participation in this group, knowing that the system functions under certain criteria of corruption," said Toño looking at Rogelio fixedly.

"You cannot or should not separate personal characteristics, from those that are systemic. Luis Echeverría and Carlos Salinas de Gortari had both: they were personally ambitious and they understood the advantages of the system perfectly. Others, like Miguel Aleman or Gustavo Diaz Ordaz, wanted to be intimidating administrators and ended up being a corrupt businessman in the case of Aleman and a murderer in the case of Diaz Ordaz," added Toño, convinced of being in the truth.

Having taken a clear position, Toño felt that he had given Rogelio an advantage that he should not have, so he continued his questioning.

"Are the actions of the Presidents selected by the PRI acceptable, taking into account the circumstances and the political system created by the Mexican Revolution?" he asked.

"In my opinion each President's performance has been a disaster. Even considering the circumstances and the political system created by the Mexican revolution, the Presidents' performance has been atrocious, to such an extent that they have achieved the complete economic collapse of the country several times over," replied Rogelio.

"But in order to understand how the Presidents accomplished this, it is necessary to unravel the system to determine which President was responsible for which part that deserves to be repudiated, and which part can be considered as being more systemic," Toño clarified.

XIII

"The one who shares and partakes gets the best take"
Popular saying.

The beginnings of the Mexican political system drew from the violence immersed in the Mexican revolution of 1910-1917. By the 1920's the large majority of the military leaders had been assassinated (among them Villa, Zapata and many more generals). In the succeeding decade, during Calles' long and influential period and the arrival of the Cardenas era, armed violence continued, this time against the Church. When Cardenas finished his term, the political system had been established and still pending conflicts were passed on to the new official party and its institutionalization. Although during President Avila Camacho time in office the Presidency was not yet the center of power, it might have become so under the influence of his brother Maximino, who, unlike the President, was a more ruthless person. Fortunately, Maximino died just before the naming of the next President, since he had already considered himself appointed.

During the Presidencies of Miguel Aleman, Adolfo Ruiz Cortines and Adolfo Lopez Mateos presidential power grew and was strengthened to the point that it was possible to violently suppress and imprison workers striking against low pay. The main concern of the Executive branch was to build an economy to be based, according to the President, on "stabilizing development" by industrializing the country through import substitution. When the Lopez Mateos period ended, the presidential office was recognized as the most important and powerful in the country. This was the result of how it handled violence and controlled the budget, but especially from the prestige pointed out by spokesmen who indicated the country's exceptional economic progress: a growing Gross Domestic Product, increasing statistics in education for most people, a life expectancy comparable to that of developed countries, and an improved newborn survival rate. And all this was achieved with very low inflation and small balance of payments deficits.

During the fifties and beginning of the sixties, the income obtained from exporting primary goods was enough to pay for valuable imports (of capital assets), as well as to cover the minimal social expenditures the government use to boast about its achievements during this period. Unfortunately, the future Presidents of Mexico would have to confront a new economic reality and a different world situation (at which they would fail terribly).

As noted above, during the fifties and early sixties the Mexican economy faced a multitude of challenges that were handled by skilled advisors, administrators and subject experts, most times under the supervisory guidelines of Presidents whose only purpose, in almost every case, was to appear authoritarian, in control, and expressing the belief that industrial development and the country's growth were the ultimate objectives. Regrettably, they were left behind by modern-day ideas regarding development. Although the rate of growth was initially positive and the foundation was laid for a sound economy, the theory of development through industrialization by import substitution was adopted, which would end tragically due to the rigid nature of the institutions born out of the Mexican revolution, the personal and inherited attitude of the country's Presidents and the prolonged time this economic doctrine was in place.

Antonio Ortiz Mena was a particularly good administrator who was heralded as an example to be followed by the PRI-supported government. He had been Finance Minister during the presidencies of Adolfo Lopez Mateos and Gustavo Diaz Ordaz, and the General Secretary of the Inter-American Development Bank from 1971 to 1988. Ortiz Mena's administration as Finance Minister was excellent and showed increasing and uninterrupted positive results in spite of the obstacles faced; however, even before this period, it was already evident that it was necessary to make some basic changes, changes that Ortiz Mena did not know how to make or could not make, and that the Presidents under whom he acted could not comprehend. It is difficult to believe that both Lopez Mateos and Diaz Ordaz accepted the idea that the economy should only produce for a small minority of the population, but that appears to be the final conclusion to be reached.

During the fifties and, especially the sixties, statistics used to represent the Mexican economy did not reflect the true situation of the country. The Gross Domestic Product was a composite number that did not indicate the sad state of agriculture or the deterioration of industries that had encountered the doors closed in foreign markets. It also did not give importance to the incredible population growth upon which the per capita Gross Domestic Product was based.

Other more accurate data were hidden by those in power. The supposed generous spending in education (which in truth had been very low) was not applied correctly since a considerable part of what appeared as current expenditures, mostly salaries, apparently corresponded to trade representatives, that is, political workers, and not to teachers.[14] It is enough to say that the results of international examinations conducted by the OCDE have given a flunking grade to all Mexican participants in international contests, then as well as in the present[15]. As for health care, as was indicated earlier, spending proudly flaunted by the government was in fact a reflection of the combined monies spent by both the government and private individuals who were directly paying to private medical professionals for their services.

The total number of Mexicans who first received the benefits of a better education and an improved quality of health care was but a minority that represented little more than 20% of the population in 1960, as noted before; however, this percentage slowly increased, despite the economic disasters, until it reached between 30% to 40% of the population in 2000.[16]

---

[14] Suspicion based on the unusual income statistics of Mexican teachers reported by the OECD showing income well above that one of every member country. See https://data.oecd.org/teachers/teachers-salaries.htm

[15] Ver PISA results in https://www.oecd.org/pisa/publications/#d.en.420737

[16] See Note 2 on page v of Introduction and refer to "Persons receiving most services" and Poverty Charts on Supplemental Statistics in this book, p. 117.

XIV

"Not everything that shines is gold"
Popular saying.

In 1970 an effort was made to increase the percentage of the population benefiting from public expenditures, but in spite of an immediate improvement, the numbers started to decrease again, as most inequality measurements would then show.

In summary, all statistics that refer to the population as a whole, in particular those that apply to the per capita population, are probably incorrect because they do not reflect the country's reality. José López Portillo and his advisors continued the mistakes and policies of his friend Luis Echeverría. His term would end, as it is well known, in the middle of out of control inflation and the nationalization of the banking sector.

From 1980 on, a large part of the rural population started to make itself felt in the cities as it began to integrate into and influence the urban middle class, considerably increasing the number of recipients of the benefits provided by the government. Even conservative Vicente Fox was forced to acknowledge that a large group of people without health insurance should be included in the health system almost for free. A hierarchical system of health care was established that worked, at least for some time, taking into account the political circumstances. Several health subsystems coexisted during this period: first, the private subsystem, which was generally of higher quality; second, the subsystem headed by the Mexican Institute of Social Security (IMSS) and the Social Services and Safety for the State Workers (ISSSTE), featuring decent quality, but having to manage too many cases; and third, the Popular Insurance subsystem, which was sometimes good and sometimes not so good, since it had to handle the most cases, including those not covered by any of the other subsystems. This still left a large part of the population without coverage.

The power of the Mexican President at the end of the fifties was centered mostly on administering the budget, recognition of the government's achievements, mostly economic, and on the use or threat of using violence through the practical and abusive utilization of intimidation.

Indeed, the government had acquired the right to discretionarily manage taxes and the federal budget, based on its victory during the revolution. From 1970 to 1985 the federation took 80% of the total national income, making state governors economically dependent on the central government. During this period, the municipalities never received more than 4% of the national budget for their expenses and depended economically, in most cases, on the governors. It could be said that state governors have never been politically or economically independent since the revolution.

The government had perfected using propaganda (in many cases paid propaganda) in its favor, and in disseminating false statistics. This is one of the main reasons why the economy seemed to be progressing without major problems during the fifties and sixties. In addition, the period following the Second World War (from 1950 to 1970) was considered to have been the golden period of capitalism, due to the growth, almost without exception, experienced by most of the capitalist countries. This also meant that other countries in the region appeared to have progressive and unproblematic economies similar to México's.

As we have indicated, Mexico had a boom period after the Second World War, and even during and after the Korean War. According to official statistics, the Gross Domestic Product (GDP) of the country grew at a rate of 5.1% during the period from 1939 to 1949 and 6.6% during the period from 1950 to 1958. Clearly the economy grew quickly, due in part to the external economic conditions and the cautious management of the economy by the government. According to official statistics the country's GDP grew without interruption from 3.56% in 1940 to 12.13% in 1980. Even if these data are not correct, there is no doubt the Mexican GDP experienced accelerated growth during those years.

In retrospect, the position of the Mexican government was excessively timid during this period, and the insistence for almost forty years on import substitution can be considered a major economic mistake. Furthermore, Mexico had to acknowledge in the nineties that closing the economy in an effort to become self-sufficient was not the best policy in a free trading world.

Even though the government has claimed success in many social programs, through several official spokespeople and the bribed press, it is clear that social expenditures by the Mexican government during the period from 1940 to 1960 were low in terms of GDP percentages, and on a continually decreasing trend until 1962, when it commenced to grow again with the adoption of external financing (although by then, while expenses were still low, it is hard to say what was their true participation). The Mexican government had inherited a visionary belief in the importance of contributing to the education and health of the population initiated during the period of Lazaro Cardenas, which some Presidents tried to follow, but others did not. In the end, although funding was allocated to both sectors in every presidential term, in no case was sufficient in comparison to international levels. These obligations were complied with by giving a few funds to the education and health sectors (mostly IMSS, ISSSTE y PEMEX), but never enough. What is known is that government expenditures helped to encourage the arrival of an avalanche of Mexicans wanting to go to school, although the funds given for education were not used to improve installations or increase teacher salaries and therefore the quality of education did not improve greatly. Likewise, these amounts did not seem to have noticeably improved the delivery of medical services, although the personnel of both private and public institutions seem to have contributed to the improvement of many of the national achievements such as the reduction of fertility in women and the newborn death rate in babies.

XV

"Become famous and you can then rest on your laurels"
Popular saying.

Unfortunately there are three additional chapters in the history of the Mexican economy under the PRI. The first chapter refers to the disproportionate population growth that the Presidents elected by the PRI allowed, and in fact stimulated. The Mexican population grew rapidly from 1940 to 1970, when it went from a total of 20.2 million in 1940 to 52.0 million in 1970, thus severely impacting all economic indicators. Mexican Presidents advocated for stimulating population growth until it became evident that a large population was not compatible with the country's economic development. By then, even though in disagreement, President Echeverría started the counteroffensive, creating the Population Council. Sadly, it was a measure that was not meant to succeed and which was implemented quite late.[17] The second chapter has to do with the immoral distribution of income that took place under the supervision of the Presidents which only benefited a small minority of the population, leaving the large majority with few opportunities and, who protested, without results, time and time again. The third chapter is a consequence of the second chapter that the Presidents supported and which resulted in the impoverishment of the countryside when they subsidized urban dwellers at the expense of rural peasants which forced them to emigrate to the cities in search of opportunities and justice.

In summary, although the Gross Domestic Product between 1940 and 1982 was not outstanding nor did it help Mexico join the countries in the developed world, it did allow the Mexican government to claim achievements with which it could weave a positive story. On the other hand, the expenses considered social expenditures under the alleged "Mexican miracle" were not exceptional, neither in the case of education nor in any other case. Truly, the

---

[17] See The National Population Council at 40 years of the Institutionalization of the Population Policy in Mexico by Carlos Welti Chanes in Scielo, Vol 20, No. 81 July/September, 2014

construction and operation of IMSS, ISSSTE and PEMEX hospitals together with infrastructure projects were not extraordinary if we consider the sums of money taxpayers made available to the government and the resulting obligations the Presidents and their assistants had with the population in general. In any case, any positive result were erased by the colossal mistake of having stimulated population growth and with the resulting overpopulation faced by cities today, and by the the shameful distribution of income that left so many people in poverty, all this without mentioning the abandonment of the countryside and the lack of opportunities the rural population had to contend with. As Miguel Székely said, referring to poverty, "The economic structure not only in Mexico but in the majority of the countries in the region generates a great inequality."[18]

Once institutionalized, the Presidents were considered the highest authority to resolve conflicts and to manage all political entities. Any attack on the political body would be countered with a response by the President exercising his power, directing every and all components of the system in the time and manner he pleased. Perhaps the most frequent exercise of power was relying on his reputation as a successful leader in the achievement of general policies, which the Presidents then transformed into exaggerated examples of their performance. This was the preferred way of operation, at least until the year 2000.

Perhaps the least important presidential approach in a conflict was to be an arbitrator, although because of the political weight of the presidency it was more a kind of compromise in which a mutual agreement was reached that the President considered fair. There being no other political option, the resolution issued in arbitration was final and usually had to be accepted by all parties. When a conflict was not resolved by arbitration, which was rare, those powers arising directly from the revolution went into play. Of course, the one most often used by Presidents and their assistants was intimidation, which was a sophisticated and very effective use of threats of violence.

The days when military commanders could do and undo were forever gone. In 1940 the case of a serviceman grabbing the wife or lover of another was not that frequent, but what was frequent was the use of intimidation with presidential approval in order to acquire private government-sponsored monopolies, or to simply bribe the press to print the version of the facts that the government wanted published. As time went by, especially during the

[18] Miguel Székely, La Desigualdad en México, mayo 1999, p. 24

Miguel Aleman period, it was common for politicians to structure public works as private businesses with the tacit support of the President. By the fifties, threats of violence and violence itself had almost disappeared from the Mexican political arena. Arrests made by Ruiz Cortines and Lopez Mateos were considered true exceptions. Violence had not existed in Mexican politics for many years, and it was evident that the government preferred not to use it. It might have been the final option to resolving a conflict in old Mexico, but it did not seem appropriate for modern times, and it most assuredly was not.

The creation of the modern state as an armed entity that could exercise power originated with Presidents Gustavo Diaz Ordaz and Luis Echeverría towards the end of the sixties and beginning of the seventies. Inside the Ministry of the Interior, paramilitary groups were formed and national army units were readied to attack protesters. Which they did.

In any case, by the early sixties there were no circumstances where the Presidents were forced to use violence against persons perceived as enemies. At no time did protesting forces attempt to modify the form or operation of the government. The Presidents in 1968 and 1970, however, reacted violently after unilaterally breaking negotiations with student protesters. Each situation was a personal decision made by the President based on personal prejudices and false expectations. The decisions of these Mexican Presidents were never systemic, but rather they were always personal, and therefore one could demand they assume full responsibility. In no way did the Presidents have the authority or the right to perpetrate the outrageous actions they committed, or to make the personal mistakes they made with the people's money.

XVI

"Madrid, Madrid in México we think a lot about you…"
Popular song.

The conversation with Rogelio had shattered Toño's steadfast belief in his arguments. The moment had arrived to face his most intimate thoughts and to decide whether what he believed in was true. He not only wanted to know whether he was correct, he wanted to focus his life and actions on what was inherently good. He thought that, after all, you live only once on this earth and he wanted to be satisfied with who he was and what he was doing with his life.

It was best to speak candidly with Rachel. He had discussed all possible topics with her, though the one on the existential reason for being had been missing. He did not know if she would be willing to have such an intimate conversation, but he would be the protagonist of the story and she would not have to share who she was or what she desired.

In his mind, however, there were several questions: why was it that countries like South Korea, Spain and China had been able to reach the status of first world countries, when Mexico has been unable to do so after so many years of progress? Why was it that there was still so much poverty in the country? Why was Mexico still an underdeveloped country?

The answers were in full view: the Mexican Presidents as leaders and the political system as the main means of implementation have been the direct reason that our people have been unable to achieve it; the few things accomplished have been thanks to the motivation of the majority of the common people in almost all cases. A long period of economic growth is clearly necessary to attain stability and economic success, but it is also important to control population growth and to ensure that there is social progress. Even though the country grew for 22 years, according to the exaggerated statistics of the PRI, its social development, that took place in spite of the government, had no direction. On the one hand, the government did not consider this important because most bureaucrats thought that the economic model based on uninterrupted growth would solve any problem; on the other hand, the population grew to such an extent, with the support of the government, that the resulting unemployment will be with us well into the future.

South Korea in 1940 was an underdeveloped country like Mexico, and still was in 1960. South Korea established its first government in 1948 and was the center of a war from 1950 to 1953. In spite of that, it has enjoyed exceptional economic growth and a vital social development during the past five decades. The income per capita grew from 1,342 in 1960 to 19,227 in 2008, and during that same period, life expectancy increased from 52.4 to 79.6 and the child mortality rate was reduced from 70 to 3.4 for each thousand newborns.

In the beginning, South Korea accepted the foreign aid offered by the United States of America. The dictator, general Park Chung-Hee, implemented a protectionist policy substituting imports to create an industrial base. The authoritarian state instituted agrarian reform and nationalized the banking sector. In the sixties, the South Korean government started its directed growth policy, changing its economic approach because of permanent inflation and large income inequality, giving it a greater involvement in the selection of preferred industries, industries under the leadership of certain families ("chaebol"). These industries eventually dominated the domestic market and became internationally competitive, to the extent that their products are known around the world.

The economic success of South Korea has been accompanied by a continuing emphasis on the education of its population and a greater participation and competitiveness in international markets. Finally, with the arrival of the sixth republic in 1987, South Korea became a democracy.

South Korea	1961	1963	1965	1967	1970	1972	1975	1977	1980
	6.8	9.2	7.1	9.1	9,9	7.2	7.8	12.3	-1.7
GDP Annual Growth %	1982	1985	1987	1990	1992	1995	1997	2000	2002
	8.3	7.7	12.5	9.8	6.2	9.5	5.9	8.9	7.7
	2005	2007	2010	2012	2015	2017	2018		
	3.9	5.8	6.4	2.4	2.7	3.2	2.6		

Sources: World Bank Group, IBRD, AID, Data. & countryeconomy.com Gross Domestic Product.

In spite of its huge population (1.386 billion in 2017) China's economy has been growing by quantum leaps for a long time. Starting in 1979, when China opened up to international trade and introduced market reforms and consequently changing the previous central planning system, until 2018 when its Gross Domestic Product (GDP) averaged 9.5%, these achievements were the result of large capital investments, since China has enjoyed an outstanding national savings rate and rapid growth in productivity due to the relocation of productive assets. According to the International Monetary Fund (IMF), China is number 73 on the list of per capita production in 2019 (ppp).

China is the number one producer of manufactured goods in the world and the largest consumer world market.

China	1961	1965	1970	1972	1975	1977	1980	1982
	-27.2	16.9	19.3	3.8	8.7	7.6	7.8	9.0
GDP Annual Growth %	1985	1987	1990	1992	1995	1997	2000	2002
	13.4	11.7	3.9	14.2	10.9	9.2	8.4	9.1
	2005	2007	2010	2012	2015	2017	2018	
	11.3	14.2	10.6	7.9	6.9	6.8	6.6	

Sources: World Bank Group, IBRD, AID, Data & Countryeconomy.com Gross Domestic Product

Spain avoided direct participation in the Second World War, but suffered a dictatorship associated with fascism from 1939 until 1975. After the war, Spain was excluded from the reconstruction programs of the European countries, experiencing an isolation that forced it to become self-sufficient. In 1940, the country had regressed to a state even worse than that of the previous decade. In 1958, the United States supported the Franco regime in exchange for setting up military bases in the country, and the government tried to reorganize itself by bringing back those individuals knowledgeable in economic matters. Despite the departure of a great number of workers, but with an economy similar to a free market one and a wave of tourism. Spain grew for years until the beginning of the seventies . The country was then able to enter the European Common market (EEC) in 1986.

Spain	1961	1965	1970	1972	1975	1977	1980	1982
	11.8	6.2	4.2	8.1	0.5	2.8	2.2	1.2
GDP Annual Growth %	1985	1987	1990	1992	1995	1997	2000	2002
	2.3	5.5	3.7	0.9	2.7	3.7	5.2	2.7
	2005	2007	2010	2012	2015	2017	2018	
	3.7	3.6	.01	-3.0	3.6	2.9	2.4	

Sources: World Bank Group, IBRD, AID, Data & Countryeconomy.com Gross Domestic Product

XVII

"I grabbed her in my arms"
Popular song.

He still remembered when he saw her pretty face for the first time. It was at a lecture, at which, as a professor he had been invited to be part of a panel to discuss the influence of the United States of America on Mexico's economy. Having arrived early, he had walked along the main hallway of the auditorium in search of the person coordinating the event, when he saw her, ticket in hand, searching for her seat. Immediately attracted to her, he had helped her to clear up her confusion, showing her to the best possible seat, one of two assigned to him in the very first row. In spite of her slight protest, he had the distinct impression that she would accept the offer from this gallant unknown person, even though not sure if his offer was genuine or not. She was surely greatly surprised when the official host expounded on Toño's credentials as one of the distinguished professors who would discuss the topic. When the event was over Rachel thanked him for his personal attention and presented her program, asking for his autograph. He scrawled it, along with his phone number, which he expected she would never use. But she called, and the telephone call was followed by a face-to-face meeting in which they shared about themselves concluding that they needed to continue to know each other even more. There was never any conflict or misunderstanding between them, and they knew that they could speak the truth without being judged. In a relatively brief time, they became intimate to the point that they appeared together at every gathering, even when they were with their families, who began to see her as the suitable person to accompany this promising young man.

Rachel had just finished her degree in Philosophy at that time, she was 23 years old, and her intelligence was as high as Toño's. Their discussions and viewpoints brought them closer together. On occasion they talked about the federal government and the benefits of working there, they seemed to be full of optimism although they had never considered in detail the government's black past, which now needed to be considered and determine what it meant in their lives.

When Toño arrived to see Rachel, he did not have to say much, since she guessed from his expression that it was something very serious and personal.

"It happens that I have discovered details from the past, and after commenting on them with my closest friends, I have become conflicted with myself," said Toño.

"What did you find out that worries you?" asked Rachel calmly.

"I found out that the government has committed many atrocities and has deceived many individuals, without genuinely pretending to benefit the people," Toño finally answered, giving his answer great importance.

"We have discussed this past record before, it has been a known fact by everyone in Mexico, and apparently it was accepted as a necessary compromise," affirmed Rachel.

"Yes, it is true we have discussed it before, and we concluded that everybody agreed to accept this government, no matter their perceived corruption, because that was the only way to survive. But it so happens that I now have discovered that there were other choices and that past Presidents were also responsible for crimes and for mismanagement, and in a certain way I feel responsible too," replied Toño.

"I believe it is a bit late for you to feel guilty now about what happened in the past," said Rachel.

"That is part of the problem, I do not feel guilty when I feel I should. Now, every time I see a ragged beggar or a poor indian selling his or her wares on the sidewalk, or a construction worker hauling bricks, I do not think they should have a better future than the one they have. But the truth is that they are not totally to be blamed for their fate; in good measure it is all of us, those of us who support this government that makes the daily decisions that affect them, who share some responsibility," stated Toño.

"If I understand you well, you are worried now because perhaps you have not been making the correct decisions. To start with, who are you to have doubts about a job which is a collective effort? In every case, the person responsible is the person who determines general policy, you are but one screw among many in that machinery," said Rachel pondering.

"That reflection is precisely what is making it difficult for me to pardon the actions of the government. If I am not the one making decisions, then the entire culpability falls on those who make those final decisions regarding the future of the country. But to be practical, let us separate what is happening today from what occurred in the past. In the past, the Presidents decided that the economic future of the country and therefore the wellbeing of its population depended on import substitution, which would allow for industrialization and economic development. It was a rational and logical choice in the thirties since it did not have the means to manage the economy nor the understanding of modern theories of underdevelopment, among other things. It was important, therefore, to follow a moderate economic policy resulting in a small deficit in the balance of payments. This was done over more than twenty years, in which excellent economists confronted capital flows coming from the United States of America and were able to keep in check the balance of payments and keep inflation low," said Toño excitedly.

"This allowed for the country to advance, and although you cannot believe the government completely, there is no doubt that the people experience economic progress during this first stage," added Rachel.

"This takes us to the period from 1962 to 2000, when the Presidents decided to embark on a type of populism that required the support of a good part of society. They only did not get it, but they also destroyed the economy and finished off the oil, the raw wealth of the people. In passing, they left the country in debt and the currency devalued," indicated Toño.

XVIII

"The one who grabs a leg kills the cow as much as the one who does it"
Popular saying.

"The big question is whether the Presidents, those who are responsible for general policy, are the only ones to be held responsible or whether their advisors should also be considered guilty when these monumental decisions are made," added Toño, sounding like an academic.

"The relationship between the Presidents and their economic advisors can shed some light on what happened and on who should bear most of the responsibility. When Lopez Mateos was nominated to be President in 1958, Antonio Ortiz Mena developed the candidate's National Economic Policy Program, Ortiz Mena was a progressive conservative politician who continued past economic policies and established the economic foundation for 'stabilizing development' in their final form. Ortiz Mena would remain as an influential politician until 1970. This economic strategy would be very successful in terms of growth, but it also coincided with the golden period of the capitalist countries and the moment when it should have been changed. This means that Gustavo Diaz Ordaz, when accepting Ortiz Mena as his economic advisor, did not even review the existing economic policy and by adopting it he committed a huge mistake. In the case of Echeverría, Leopoldo Solís, Director of the Central Bank, and one of his main advisors, describes how Echeverría preferred foreign debt to a tax proposal that the private sector had already rejected," Toño exclaimed.

"Other advisors seemed to have influenced the final decisions of the Presidents, both formally in their proposals as government officials, or informally as personal friends. In these cases, there is no question that when a government official's proposal is turned into policy, he should be held responsible together with the President, like in the case of Ortiz Mena, but if his proposal is rejected, he should most likely resign from his position as a public official. However, if the advisor is part of a clique of politicians who are members of the power elite, that even if their ideas are rejected will be rewarded for their loyalty by being appointed to a politically neutral position or by being awarded some other distinction. These advisors obviously belong

64

to a leadership group opposed to the common people and should definitely be held responsible. It is difficult to evaluate the position of key Mexican main economic advisors, but clearly most of them, Ministers as well as other top public officials, belonged to the group in power and therefore are as guilty as the Presidents. In every case, however, it is the President himself who is directly responsible for not only economic, but general policy as well," concluded Toño.

"Nevertheless," Toño continued, "there is always the point of view of the government. The Presidents and their advisors will surely argue that they did not know about the lies the government disseminated, and in any case economic policy is always defensible based on the lack of knowledge about its end results and on the uncertainty of its concepts. It was impossible to know if an economic policy adopted by a President was going to end up in economic disaster after many years, as in this case. Initially, the Mexican economy was only about avoiding price increases and inflation, later it was thought that growth was a fundamental concern and that the balance of payments deficits should be avoided. To benefit the population by providing services was never seriously considered."

"Unfortunately, the Presidents and their economic advisors, even if they refuse to accept responsibility, must admit they had enough time to change direction and to learn about the lies spread by them for so many years. It was basically a matter of realizing that the country should not remain isolated, especially if it was understood that foreign influences had a vital impact on the national economy. If anyone could and should have known that, it was the economic advisors."

"There is also the question of criminal activity. In Mexico's case most if not all the population accepted the PRI regime under the false impression of the country's progress. The reality was different, but even without taking this into consideration, when the government is the protagonist of criminal acts that cannot be accepted under any circumstance it is necessary to reject them. Unconditional support of the government after it shows its true criminal nature is not possible. The government belongs then to an illegal group and there is no other option but to denounce the government's illegal actions, even if it benefits some of the people. Even if a criminal government survives for a long time or carries on actions proper of a legitimate government, it will always be criminal and illegal."

"There is still another critical question open for discussion. Up to what point would you say that someone hired as a government employee for a department handling economic affairs is responsible for the measures taken under his supervision?" asked Toño.

"I believe the answer is going to depend on the specific program you are talking about, but in no way you can assign total responsibility to someone who has only developed or directed part of an economic program. You cannot attribute any responsibility to someone who is executing something he believes is a good plan," responded Rachel intelligently.

"If I interpret this statement logically, it means that I am not responsible for something I believe it is a good plan; however, I might be held, at least partially, responsible for an economic program I do not approve of if I have developed or directed with others," replied Toño.

"But to adopt an attitude like that would complicate your job terribly. The purpose of government is to make the necessary decisions to achieve the wellbeing of everyone. If a particular decision is aimed or not toward this objective is in many cases a matter of opinion," added Rachel.

"Well in the first place, I believe that governance is an effort to benefit all the people you oversee; when that is not the direction being taken, it is the obligation of an employee to openly state his or her disagreement, and to resign if the complaint is not addressed with an explanation of how it will benefit all the population," indicated Toño, reflecting on what Rachel had said.

"Of course, there are times when it is not perfectly established if an adopted policy will be beneficial or not; in such cases, is appropriate for the employee to continue to carry out policies until it can be determined with certitude whether it is beneficial or not," said Toño. "It could very well be that a policy does not benefit the public in the short term, but that could it benefit it in the long run, especially when economic in nature. In the case of Mexico, the government has often not been focused on benefitting the majority. The government said it was, but that was not true. The government was, especially immediately after an election, a job placement office, and that was the way many bureaucrats looked at it, without considering the pillaging that took place, mostly by highly-placed bureaucrats, and the generalized pilfering common in most areas," added Toño.

"Despite that description of the Mexican government, it does not apply to all bureaucrats many of whom provide a service which Mexicans citizens and the Mexican government have relied on time and time again. There have always been bureaucrats whose diligence, knowledge and dedication have facilitated the efficient functioning of the government, but they are in the minority in the case of Mexico. That being so, the determination of whether a government acts or not for the benefit of society will depend on its policy, their implementation and the final results," said Rachel, countering Toño.

"Accepting that the government in general did not provide benefits for the majority in the past, there are many bureaucrats who enclosed themselves in their positions, forming a massive and oppressive institution not easy to break down. Some Mexican government institutions certainly have not been far from this description. On the other hand, if most employees support the continuance of an adverse entity such as a government that does not benefit society, how can you not assign responsibility to these employees?" asked Toño.

"In any case, you apply the concept that a government exists to benefit its population. That way, if it does not do so for whatever reason or circumstance, you can refer to it as an inept or illegal government," concluded Rachel.

XIX

"When you stand next to a good tree, good shelter you receive"
Popular saying.

"Let us say I participate in a devaluation like the one that took place in 1995, at the end of the period of Carlos Salinas de Gortari's term and the beginning of Ernesto Zedillo's, when there were in principle several options that could have solved the financial imbalance in the current account. However if the government handles it ineptly, as it did at that time, I only have two available alternatives: to attempt to solve the problem by sharing what I know or to detach myself from the government, arguing that I cannot participate in an inept operation." Toño pointed out.

"Taking into consideration your example, yes, you have only two options, and whichever one you choose you must do so with certainty," emphasized Rachel.

"This makes me answer the second question in a more personal and concrete way: in today's circumstances, taking into account the economic mess left behind by former Presidents, should I in the presence of a case of ineptitude impose my version of the path Mexico should follow, or should I just quit?" asked Toño, wondering what his next step should be.

"An attitude like that would imply that you are an influential intellectual in national economic matters who should be taken into account, which is not likely true," said Rachel, touching lovingly Toño's shoulder.

"Even if I am not, my personal stand does count when deciding whether I want to remain in the government or not," replied Toño quickly.

"I do not think that is true, unless you had an exceptional solution to the problem that you would be willing to sell to your colleagues," clearly affirmed Rachel.

"But there is another way to disagree with the economic policy of the country: when you do not agree with integrating the national economy into the capitalist system," said Toño.

"Which in the case of Mexico, being a next-door neighbor to the most capitalist country in the world, is not an idea that would be accepted, for now, without the intervention of the United States of America. It is simply not a practical position," insisted Rachel.

"It is clear, returning to the main question, that you are assuming that the current government is inept. I, on the other hand, would say that in truth the government has never been inept because in every case it has had high-level advisors," continued Rachel.

"It is difficult to say that the advice given was top-level advice when Mexico has fallen into these economic crises that someone with a minimum knowledge of economics could have prevented. It is not difficult to explain what happened in 1976 under Luis Echeverría, or in 1982 under Jose Lopez Portillo, or even in 1994 during the period of Ernesto Zedillo," said Toño, raising his voice.

"True, but not everything can be explained in economic terms, nor does everything that happens belong to the economic world. A government is a very complex institution, made up of many elements, and although an explanation may appear to be simple and clear, it most probably is not," argued Rachel.

"Let us review what happened. Even though Diaz Ordaz had it easy since all he had to do was let Antonio Ortiz Mena take the helm of his 'stabilizing development,' he is, nevertheless, responsible for accepting this economic policy and for using foreign money until it reached an unthinkable amount for that time. As for Miguel de la Madrid, who knew about economics, he exemplified the obedient, slow, and steady President. His economic and political policy, which in accordance with the American prescription could not be any different, consisted of moderating and limiting measures, without any apparent concern for the people. His fight against inflation was relatively successful, he reduced the participation of the government in the economy by introducing the principles of the trend known as 'neoliberal' which started opening up the economy, and he professed to support free trade," reflected Toño.

"The case of Luis Echeverría is one for a medical psychiatrist more than for an economist or a political scientist. Surely Hugo B.Margain, Leopoldo Solís, Julio Rodolfo Moctezuma and many others tried to deter the President in his efforts to base the economy and his 'shared development' entirely on foreign loans, but his personal style and his megalomania put an end to these efforts," he added.

"Similarly, you can also say that Jose Lopez Portillo lost his sense of reality after being treated like a king for years," added Rachel, who after a pause continued. "The case of Carlos Salinas de Gortari is strange but it can be explained. Anxious to be legitimately accepted by the Mexican people, since he obtained the presidency by means of what was said to be a fraudulent election, Salinas de Gortari headed the so-called 'technocrats' and introduced huge changes into the Mexican economy following neoliberal principles. Unfortunately, together with Ernesto Zedillo, who succeeded him as President, ended up like his predecessors, with a currency devaluation and an economic and political crisis."

"On the other hand, it is almost inconceivable to think that a President does not want to benefit the population under his care in some way, however, it is quite different to establish that his actions will benefit all of them, or at least will benefit the majority. In these cases we are talking about Presidents who perhaps thought they could do good things, but lost their way when faced by the many obstacles they had to overcome and who ended up destroying the economy and hurting everyone," exclaimed Toño, who continued, "In conclusion, it is clear that since the power given to Mexican Presidents was practically absolute, it weakened the decision-making process and, in spite of having advisors, these were usually unable to alter a decision made by the President, although at times they were able of providing content, thereby influencing many situations."

"Miguel de la Madrid as well as Carlos Salinas de Gortari and Ernesto Zedillo were trained in the United States of America and their leanings regarding economic matters were well known. All of them acted in accordance with principles learned abroad, and at least in the cases of Miguel de la Madrid and Ernesto Zedillo, there is the clear suspicion that the Americans greatly influenced them," finished Toño.

"As a matter of fact, regarding the presidential advisors, there were many individual differences in their understanding of economic matters. It is difficult to disqualify an economist who advocates a given theory or economic model. Similarly, economists should not lose their impartiality for relying on questions that are merely technical. However, the political and economic life of the country demands that everyone, including economists, clearly state their position before the facts and before the people in the political and economic arena," reflected Toño. "If you are part of the governing elite, even as an economist, you are in a way part of the decisions made, unless of course you publicly disavow them."

"As far as I am concerned, I must conclude that my conscience must be at peace since, unless I have something fundamental to contribute, in which case

I will either make my expertise available to my employer or I will resign, I want to make sure the government works for the benefit of the majority either in the short or the long term," said Toño.

The discussion was over, conclusions were clear, and his personal position as far as the government was concerned, was safe. The government was honest and dedicated to the betterment of most of the people. As an important advisor, Toño could dedicate himself to the execution of his duties without being afraid of being on the wrong side. He had surely benefited many and his area operated in the right direction.

XX

"He who runs with wolves, learns to howl"
Popular saying.

Although he wished next Sunday would not arrive, the day did arrive.

The gathering, normally full of young people, was packed that day, to the point that chairs from other rooms had to be brought in so everyone could sit. Toño started his talk without a preamble, without presentation, and without any fuss.

"As I promised, in this session I am going to explain the position of the Mexican government concerning the events that provoked the resounding fall of the national economy. In the first place, I have to say that leadership in economics and politics, and this I know from experience, is neither easy nor simple, but rather it is difficult and complicated," Toño stated.

"In 1930, the Mexican government was trying to protect the country from the Great Depression that had followed the fall of the American stock exchange in 1929. There were great feuds among the economists of the time regarding the best way to get out of the quagmire, which it was not easy since the Mexican economy was also depressed, and many of the economic tools that exist now were either unavailable or not known: it was a different reality. The exchange rate was fixed and linked to the gold-standard, and the central bank showed no influence nor leadership. That said, the final decision depended on a President who did not understand much about the economy. Fortunately for the country, a distinguished economic advisor imposed himself who was able to lead the economy out of the great depression and to establish an expansionist policy that was criticized in the beginning."

"In 1940, the Mexican economy returned to normal, which was the exportation of minerals and agricultural products and, for the first time since the revolution, the government was engaged in growing the Gross Domestic Product (GDP) above all else. General Lazaro Cardenas, who was President from 1936 to 1941, is the exception to the absence of great statesmen during the country's recent history. Not only did he achieve the expropriation of oil, but he also effectively undertook land distribution, created the political party which would rule the country's future, and instituted the six-year Presidency, ousting Plutarco Elias Calles. Advanced by Eduardo Suarez, his position regarding economic matters was one of expansionism, and major works of infrastructure were carried out. There was also an important discussion taking place regarding the role of the state in the economy of the country. Theories held among economists during this time indicate that a government like the Mexican government should focus on economic development above all, which meant the increase in industrial production. The Mexican government finally adopted the idea of import substitution and industrial development as something clearly viable and logical."

"Starting in 1940 Mexico entered a very conducive period for political and economic growth, although neither of these two aspects would be taken advantage of for the benefit of the people. In political matters, the corporatism introduced by Cardenas spread into every political institution, turning them into rigid entities unable to respond to the people's needs. On the other hand, the economy seemed to have found the best way to reach the goals of continuous industrial growth. Unfortunately, neither the official party (PRI) nor the economy responded to the real needs of the people: the official party would become atrophied in its practices and would exclude any other political entity; the economy would show growth, but the results be tarnished by the government's exalting these statistics, and the statistics would concentrate on production data, ignoring the real needs of the people."

"Both politics and the economy would start to crumble in the sixties, after the economy had showed almost uninterrupted growth since 1940, until totally collapsing during the period from 1968 to 2000, at which time the Presidency passed to the conservative party (Partido Acción Nacional, PAN), who had no idea as to what to do."

"In summary, that is the past we were destined to have. The question now is: to what extent is the current government responsible for this past? Probably not much, since in the first place those who are now part of the government were not a part of it back then; second, those who held, or who still hold, the same ideas should not be part of any future governments; and third, those who led the government in the wrong direction are responsible if they did not fight for different choices or did not quit the government when it became clear that its ideas were going to fail," continued Toño.

"It is true that it is the Presidents who are ultimately responsible, since they were in charge and it was their task to make decisions. The presidential advisors were important, and we know that although they did not have the last word, their opinions influenced the decisions made by the Presidents. After the excellent job carried out by Eduardo Suarez for two six-year presidential terms, the national economy was managed by Mario Beteta and Antonio Carrillo Flores, who both endorsed the economic policy of import substitution during a time that was apparently appropriate for it. Other advisors were not as fortunate and some, in contrast, had to pay for their influence. Hugo B. Margain ended up resigning during President Echeverria's term because he disagreed with how the economy was being managed, mismanagement which led to the 1976 devaluation. David Ibarra and Jesus Silva Herzog Flores had to shoulder mistakes made under the six-year term of Jose Lopez Portillo, who was greatly influenced by Andres de Oteyza and Carlos Tello. Jaime Serra Puche also had to resign due to the errors committed during the six-year term of Ernesto Zedillo. Julio Rodolfo Moctezuma had to resign due to his constant clashes of opinion with Carlos Tello (Minister of Budget and Programing), but Pedro Aspe Armella, however, provided leadership that lasted Salinas de Gortari's entire term, despite the economic results."

"Let me tell you a little about the influences and the conditions that surround a person working in the offices that handle economic issues. It is an environment with a lot of pressure. The important matters are handled by the main employees, these advisors hope that their ideas would be presented to the President. Although in many cases these ideas were discussed by other employees, they were never criticized mostly because criticism in Mexico is taken as a personal attack that must be avoided."

"In the seventies and eighties, the direction of the economy was heatedly discussed, but again without criticism. Presidents Luis Echeverria and Jose Lopez Portillo had the advantage of having good advisors, but their ultimate decisions were terribly wrong. The Mexican environment has always suffered from a multiplicity of opinions that never reach the President, due on the one hand to the President's personality and on the other to the rigidity of a system that prevents the infiltration of opinions contrary to those of the regime, and thus not allowing other options to be considered, even those which were by then clearly viable alternatives."

"Once having decided which model would be implemented, the advisor and the President were committed to following it and to justifying their choice. Based on these decisions, it became necessary to coordinate the economy and politics in such a way as to not deviate from the objectives established. Generally, most of the Ministries that handled economic issues would clash with those handling political matters. For example, attaining a high rate of industrial productivity clashed with the artificial suppression of worker's salaries, the lack of foreign currency to pay for the necessary importation of capital goods was coming directly from the application of subsidies given to the countryside. Above all, if the increase in prices were allowed, it would result in a high rate of inflation and, independently of the real lowering of salaries, interest rates would soar. Furthermore, analysts were the ones to decide which were the final figures to be used for aggregate demand, national aggregate supply, imports, exports, saving totals and national and foreign investment amounts. These and many other considerations were part of the daily tasks of these employees and supervisors. To work as an economic advisor to a President requires trust in the political and economic members of the government, in spite of the overgrown Mexican bureaucratic sectors. That clearly did not happen during the crises in the seventies, eighties and nineties."

"As you all know the system suffered collapses in 1976, 1982 and 1994, to mention just those dates when the imbalance between the economy and politics was clear for everyone to see."

"Now, I again ask, were the advisors and employees as guilty as the Presidents? Are employees currently working in the government guilty for a system that has been corrupt for decades?" insisted Toño.

XXI

"You know better than anyone that you failed me"
Popular song.

"Who can say with conviction that there are not at least two ways of looking at the development of a country? The one followed by the Presidents and their advisors, and the one not followed by them. Let me ask you again, what course of action would you follow if you had to decide? The well-known beaten path that is slowly heading towards certain failure, or the unknown and exciting path which may be full of dangers, but is heading towards new and potentially more successful results. The first is the one taken by the Presidents we vilify; the second is the one that would be taken by everyone who has criticized the economic development that has been followed." He believes that, in retrospect, we can do better than the Presidents did, or, better said, a true statesman could do it better than they did.

"I have already mentioned that during the period from 1940 to 1980 there were several different theories regarding the development of an underdeveloped country. Initially, the idea of import substitution was the most viable (and less costly) to attain uninterrupted and sustainable production. Soon this theory changed from concentrating on the growth of the Gross Domestic Product to one where the State became the benefactor's population, thus highlighting the focus on public expense. This change, the result of the direct influence of developed countries, does not affect Mexican politics fully until the seventies, when, thanks to foreign credit, it is finally possible to consider allocating important sums of money to social benefits."

"The performance of Antonio Ortiz Mena, already mentioned, has been overly praised by PRI supporters. He did not start to turn the economy around when he should have, by emphasizing issues that obviously required his attention. Yes, in effect, at the end of his tenure he pointed out that some changes were needed, but these changes referred to a time prior to his term and to the people, ordinary people who he only thought of as demographic data. His successful policy of concentrating on stable growth will always be praised, but at the same time he will always be criticized for setting aside the equitable income distribution for the population at large, as well as for his required loyalty to the Presidents. If you think that the lack of a fair distribution of income and a decent education is exaggerated, see what was done in South Korea on these matters in the sixties and seventies."

"The Mexican system has never had a sufficiently independent and outstanding economic advisor or thinker who could create his own objectives and models to guide the national economy. Lately, the economists who have molded the national economic institutions have been influenced by concepts developed mostly in the United State of America, which can be inferred from their academic affiliations. Although no one had shown the intellectual fortitude to forge a different course, Leopoldo Solis does stand out recently, guiding Presidents and other advisors from the Central Bank and the office of the President. His merits, mistakes and connections to the PRI elite have motivated much discussion around economic and political topics in Mexico."

"Now, let us look at the question of responsibility and the ambiguity regarding government advisors and employees. Those who participated in important decisions, such as the 1976 devaluation which was impossible to stop due mainly to Echeverria's refusal to insist on a fiscal package that the business community did not want, automatically became accomplices of the President. All economic advisors were surely aware of this situation in advance, and should have taken the necessary steps to quit the Executive Power. Those who for personal circumstances could not do so should have at least expressly stated their opposition. Most advisors, therefore, should have dissociated themselves from those policies they did not agree with. Of course, this is easier said than done, however, the presidential team should have been dismantled before committing such a serious error. As an example, Hugo B. Margain was able to do it, although a consummate member of the power elite. As for the employees who knew what was happening, unlike their bosses, they needed their jobs to survive and you can hardly find them guilty for remaining at their posts. An act of rebellion by an employee could be seen as a display of true courage, but up to a certain point that employee would be risking unnecessary reprisals."

"In a country like Mexico during past decades it was almost impossible to find an educated person who did not belong to the group in power or who was not associated with it in some way. There were a few arenas for action and these were small. Nevertheless, the areas open to the private sector and to companies not belonging to the government, as well as those belonging to the education sector, were constantly expanding. Those who decided not to join the government led a poor, but still eventful and satisfactory life."

"The occasions when advisors who held different ideas from those of the Presidents were rare, or were almost never brought up in public. A politician who wanted to reach great highs would with difficulty question the prevailing ideas, even if world circumstances had changed. To think differently, in both economic and political matters, was not encouraged and should be avoided at any cost because it produced division and strife. At that time, the thinking was that shared beliefs were conducive to progress, which is what all Mexicans wanted."

"And yet, political and economic theory can only be born in an environment of contradiction and renewal. A struggle between monetarist and structuralist supporters took place in Mexico during this period, with the victorious group clearly excluding the other from power, and from access to the President's ear. It was not until Miguel de la Madrid's presidency, when the President himself was an economist, that the fight to exclude others was ultimately won, with the resulting economic and political downfall."

"The adoption of an economic and political theory is a necessity for modern societies: which one would be the most appropriate one for today's Mexico? That is an answer that a true statesman would provide, without excluding the debate around and contribution of many possible solutions." The answers and opinions were so many in response to this question, that the session ended without a clear winner. But Toño was satisfied; his considerations and questions had provoked a great reaction among the young people in attendance. He did not feel guilty, nor did he feel that he belonged to a corrupt organization; his work was legitimate. Yet he still saw the signs of economic disaster in the faces of the people.

XXII

"The robe does not make the monk"
   Popular saying.

Without commenting or saying anything, Toño left the gathering without even saying goodby to anyone. He suddenly felt a great sadness enveloped him, and he desired some solitude and to be left alone. Perhaps he just needed to walk a little and soon he would feel better.

Walking aimlessly did not make him feel any better, however. The sensation he was feeling formed a lump in his throat, but he could not figure out what it was exactly. However, he instantly knew what he was feeling when a small girl of no more than six approached him to offer the few packages of chewing gum still left in her small box. Her dark little face was smeared with city street ashes and dirt and her eyes were playful and full of life. Toño could not hold it in anymore and his tears started to violently hit the sidewalk's pavement. The little girl, without understanding why, slowly moved away from Toño, as if he were a sick starving dog.

The catharsis made him feel better but showed him that his soul had not forgiven him entirely, in fact he knew then that he would never be free of the accusation he had seen in those black eyes, so innocent and yet victims of an immorally formed government and terrible leaders. In how many houses, he thought, were people calmly eating without wanting to see how this pretty little girl was unknowingly being victimized by them for having been born in the wrong place and in the wrong social class. How many victims wander through the city, amid the hustle and bustle and at the end of the day, huddle wherever they can, without protection, hoping the night won't be too cold, in an effort to try to survive one more day. He still remembered the handful of boys, almost children, crammed like bunches of fruit around the openings of the ventilation ducts of the city's metro, hoping to catch some of the heat generated by the trains.

With a sad expression on his face he walked among the many stands of food, clothing, counterfeit items, and the endless variety of articles which constituted the growing illicit street trade that provided a source of income for all the unemployed in the huge city, and which obstructed the passage of pedestrians seeking the entrance of the city's metro train.

"My tears are not enough, he thought, an enormous wave of indignation and its accompanying power are needed to fix these huge catastrophes that but a few humans have caused. It is impossible to judge an entire system and all those who are a part of it, but if there was any justice, although not a Mexican value for now, all the elements making up the system would be found guilty."

"The justification, naturally, would be that it was not done intentionally, that the Presidents did not know the economy would be so unpredictable, and that someone had to do it. In any case they followed their instincts, experience and knowledge, which were as good or better than those of anyone else. If the results had not been outstanding, surely others would have achieved just the same, or maybe even worse results. Managing a government is a complex and difficult task. True, the flow of money, so much money, causes human beings to feel so much power that it is difficult for them to resist the temptation to impose their will on others. Technical expertise in how to manage the government is not the main problem, but fairness when allocating funds is. Furthermore, everything depends on an advisor who hopefully has studied the consequences of the decisions being made. The question is not so much who will receive a certain sum of money, but who is capable of carrying out the work to completion. How can you reduce the number of poor people in a country? We already know that focusing on economic growth is an important factor, but it is not enough; inflation must be minimal and the balance of payments trade deficit must be small or compensated somehow, income distribution must be equitable and health care and education must be provided. Surely, the best way to address the issue is by allocating enough money to programs designed to eradicate poverty and to the programs supporting these expenditures which would surely improve the standard of living of every citizen's and the quality of their participation in the development and progress of the country."

Toño talked to himself out loud, "all you Mr.Presidents, knew that you were playing with human lives and yet you never consider putting the people above everything else, as the evidence clearly shows one to so say it. It was obvious that you were not statesmen; nevertheless, you assumed this role as if you were. You never understood that your mistakes could end up in the death of someone, maybe many. You never boarded a city bus like ordinary folks do to see the reality surrounding you. Some of you were even recruited by foreign powers as informants.[19] It is possible to criticize your advisors as well, although their culpability can be mitigated since their advice was based on technical reasons, and they were not properly prepared to give advice, even when they believed they were. Their knowledge had been developed by others using foreign concepts. Someone other than yourselves, Mr. Presidents, should have made the decisions needed to develop this society, others would have known what to do. You have enjoyed great advantages, but you have wasted them. You should be ashamed."

"After you have vacated the presidency, when I come in, I will continue to be the face of the government, but in spite of that I cannot do anything to redress your wrongs, I must live with your reputation and your mistakes. There is nothing I can do about this, but my performance cannot sink to your level nor can it depend on a system that would allow me to do whatever I want without retribution. Many of your advisors still practice with the outdated tools that caused them to fail, others, less confused, are now beginning to build a new order that is relevant only to Mexico."

"I know that there is no tomorrow to make decisions for those who demand a solution to the country's problems today; I know that to lead a country is complex and demanding. Yet you have had money, a lot of money, and time, a lot of time, to find a solution to the country's underdevelopment. I know that we have always found an innovative and authentic way to lead our people, and this is no different. Other societies have accomplished it, now it is our turn."

Toño continued thinking and talking to himself. People started to look at him as if he were an odd individual, as if suddenly they realized that he was not behaving normally.

[19] Everything seems to indicate that Presidents Adolfo Lopez Mateos, Luis Echeverria Alvarez and Gustavo Diaz Ordaz were CIA informants. See https://tuul.tv/en/politics-and-blogs/mexican-presidents-who-were-agents-cia

XXIII

"I went up to the room where the crime took place…"
Popular song.

It was at that time that Toño immersed himself in handling the economic and political problems from his position at the center of the federal government. The struggle for political power passed before his eyes every day and he could see how the protagonists were seizing all possible resources to attain a decisive advantage, from taking advantage of relatives and friends to bribing journalists. Everything was acceptable when it came to political matters.

The days had been passing unnoticed, the routine making their jobs somewhat boring, when a yellowish document, which should not have been there, landed on top of his desk. It was a telegraphic confirmation addressed to the President's office. Considering it unimportant he tossed it to one side and continued to analyze the stack of files he needed to complete. He could not, however, get the image of this yellowish paper in his office out of his mind.

The next day, he decided to study the document that surely was delivered to his office by mistake and most likely referred to a transaction of which he already had a record of on his files. Without delay, Toño hurried to his office that morning to read the document carefully. As he suspected, once he saw the confirmation, it was a confidential transaction that should have never come to his office that documented money transactions, records which should be in a file in his office but under an assumed name. Although he immediately thought of conferring with his friend and boss, Anibal, he decided to investigate further before undertaking any consultations.

Encountering one surprise after another, the document led him to uncover the creation, under his very nose, of a foreign fund belonging, no more and no less, to the President himself. (It was a very-well done simulation his office would have ignored). It was clear that the transactions had been hidden for a long time and that several public officials had acted as accomplices. Toño thought that the discovery of such a huge crime should, for now, stay hidden from the public, until a decision was made about what to do with such remarkable information.

Toño understood that the immensity of his discovery demanded he take a personal stand, which meant either his permanent submission to the system, or his defiance and subsequent exclusion from it. At first, he wanted to let his close coworkers know, but he later reflected that it was too important a discovery to be shared; besides, he thought, it was something so serious that it could eventually put his confidants in danger. As far as he was concerned, his position in the national bureaucracy was solid. Although there were other political and economics intellectuals, almost no one had Toño's background and seniority and most especially no one enjoyed the admiration and friendship of all his coworkers. For now, the best action to take was to be silent.

The work in the office was, to a certain extent, monotonous, but the problems that had to be resolved were not. Frequently Toño, Ovidio, Manuel or Rogelio had to stay overtime to find a solution to a problem; you could say that none of them had fixed working hours.

In the mornings, though not too early, Toño sometimes used to have breakfast in a regular restaurant, unlike other public officials who preferred the elegance and decorum of expensive places. However, Toño and his guests, frequently his close coworkers, chose popular places frequented by ordinary folks. Toño felt more comfortable there, though not Ovidio and Rogelio. Toño insisted, nonetheless, that it was especially important not to lose contact with the average citizen, even if they only handled impersonal and dehumanized accounts. After all, the money passing through their fingers was almost always the people's money, the money of those seating at the other tables while they ate breakfast.

A description of their routine tasks defied any order or principle. Toño, occasionally had to find out what tasks should be tackled, taking into account what had happened recently, but most of the time they audited what other Departments or Ministries had done. Sometimes money that was missing was confirmed, or the amounts indicated by the person in charge did not match the accounting established for his or her unit. In any case, any dispute was to be handled by the political operatives, who would determine whether the reasons were valid or whether an appropriate political explanation should be attached. In no case would the public officials under Toño know the final resolution of a disputed issue. Nevertheless, Toño followed each important case and he would discuss them with his superior, his friend Anibal, the flashy Minister of Auditing, whose work consisted in examining any discrepancy and leaving in the hands of the Minister of Finance everything that remained unresolved. You could say that the eyes of the President himself scanned every document passing through Toño's hands at the Department of Auditing and the Ministry of Finance.

The reality of the political structure was that the important jobs, those paying more and requiring that their holders make important political decisions, were in the hands of a few, well-connected individuals, who formed a small clique or inner circle around the President and who, as the main group of leaders, obeyed the guidelines issued by the President. Political loyalty was absolutely necessary in order to aspire to a position of trust, and solid specialized knowledge began to be required as well, to attain a high rank within the party. Little by little unknown politicians with not known militancy, began to be appointed to positions that would normally have been given to traditional politicians. The fight for power became more open and sometimes more public.

In fact, one of the characteristics of national politics was the dispute over public government positions, even if they were unimportant. Any public official, once having reached a certain level, should expect some politicking, ranging from complaints to his superiors to elaborate schemes to make public his faults to remove him, or at least, to not allow him to continue to ascend the government hierarchy. The correct strategy was to join a strong group and contribute to the deceptions and falsehoods against the most promising public officials. In this order of ideas, those placed in important positions were not always the best choices, but on the contrary, they were those with greatest creativity, and those with the most skill at circumventing the attacks of others.

Finally, after some time has passed and after much thought, Toño reached the conclusion that his close coworkers and colleagues should learn about the circumstances they were working under and what kind of people their bosses truly were. Ignoring the great responsibility he himself had shouldered, he decided to let his trusted team formed by Ovidio, Manuel and Rogelio, know that their President was a thief without scruples, that he had found foreign money transfers and a false account that without a doubt was owned by the head of the Executive branch. After firmly telling them what he had discovered and the finality of his conclusions, the confession proved so shocking, that no one said anything for a moment. Toño took advantage of their silence to remind them that this information was strictly confidential and that it should be shared with no one. His colleagues then asked him details about what he had discovered. Step by step Toño showed them what he had found, from the confirming telegraph until how he discovered the connection to the President. And he assured them that there was more, not only about the President but also about some of his close associates, who were not only trying to deceive them, but to deceive the country, its institutions and its people, as well.

The next step to be considered was to determine whether they should or could remain in their jobs, knowing what they knew and now that they had unwillingly become the President's accomplices. The categorical answer as far as Toño was concerned was a NO, he would not stay in his position since he considered the government corrupt and he was not willing to be part of a criminal enterprise. It was not a difficult decision to reach, although Toño had worked a good number of years in the public sector and his reputation had been well earned. His untimely exit was surely to raise many questions among political commentators and experts about the government. His answer for now would be that he was exhausted from such intense work and that it was time to find less strenuous work. In view of the fact that his close co-workers knew every detail, as well as his stand on the matter, their position would be pending for now. It was not necessary to ask them for an immediate decision.

He of course, consulted with Rachel, about this huge personal decision. She was totally in agreement, and she advised that he let most of his many coworkers know the terms of his resignation, but not the real reason. It was necessary to do things with great care, since the other employees would personally find themselves in a serious predicament should they know the truth. Toño should not create a situation that might lead to mass resignations which then would have to be explained. Besides, if the great majority of workers did know nothing they would continue to work with the understanding that they were doing it for the public good, and somehow that would be true.

XXIV

"The mouth of a blabber falls sooner than a cripple"
Popular saying.

In solidarity, Ovidio and Rogelio resigned also immediately in the same gathering where they had been informed of the mess, in spite of the time Toño had given them after he had announced what the President had done. In each case the reason for their resignation was neither mentioned, nor asked for. Of course, everybody assumed it was a normal movement of public officials, after years of service, but the President and the Minister Anibal knew that something had caused their departure, and they were worried. Their suspicion was justified when Toño, after thirteen years as a government bureaucrat, started writing articles about the economic policies of the regime for the magazine *El Porvenir*.

His articles, intelligent and well thought out, appeared in an almost unknown publication supported by the presence of a well-known intellectual. Despite the passage of time, the publication had never become popular, perhaps because of its professed intellectual pedigree, or perhaps because of its editorial approach, or perhaps because of its lack of channels of distribution. But though the publication was almost unknown, its arguments and reasonings reached all mass media and their readers and supporters. The magazine's stance was somewhat paradoxical. Although typically Mexican, it proclaimed the virtues coming from the western countries, in particular the United States of America. In its pages reference was also made of the endemic corruption of the government, almost always referring to mostly not federal, minor public officials and the absence of justice, the lack of holding powerful people accountable to rules, and the continuing cases of unpunished abuses.

The government tolerate criticism up to a point, reckoning that it was a fair exercise of democracy, but beyond that the magazine was not permitted to talk and even less to publish written text.

El Porvenir was published thanks to the courage of its personnel, but it's articles put the magazine at the center of much controversy and its license was always in danger, always dependent on the government. As for the general public, Toño's transfer from being a bureaucrat to becoming an author in a

86

critical magazine passed unnoticed, but in government circles it was treated as a change of major significance. The President and Anibal's concerns were not the only clues that he departed without a clear explanation of the reason for his separation from his position. Many public officials lamented losing such a valuable and experienced person, and yet some expressed that although Toño was likely to respect his knowledge of certain governmental affairs in accordance with the law, his value was such that it was not possible to let him go without giving him a good reason to not to divulge what he had learned because the level of his position. It was clear that many politicians were afraid that their peccadilloes would appear in the press. The President, however, had a different and greater fear: having among his close colleagues a true enemy who would now need to be destroyed.

Of course, from the outset Toño had assumed , together with his friends later, that the political consequences of his discovery would place him among the enemies of the President and of his friend Anibal. Considering the circumstances, it was necessary to be sure. Without thinking much about it anymore, he spoke confidentially to his friend Anibal.

"This is something that is sinister and against all what we consider sacred," Toño said, trying to anticipate his friend's answer."

"I know that in the end you too will be deeply affected by this, and I am going to need your protection," he added.

"The President has deceived us, he is not the person we had hoped he would be and the people do not matter to him," said Toño without giving Anibal time to answer.

"I do not know what to say to all this," responded Anibal defensively.

"As you know, I have already come to a decision; however, my armor is very weak without your support. You should probably not let the President know that you know his secret," indicated Toño.

Baffled by what he had just heard, Anibal rushed to leave the place where they had met and was soon lost in the chaotic traffic of the city.

Managing the country was a complex task, and the President did not seem to take his role very seriously; nevertheless, Toño's resignation was something he definitely should worry about.

"Do you realize that Antonio is publishing in *El Porvenir*?" asked the President.

"Yes, I know. I'll take care of this little problem," replied Anibal.

"It had better be soon," replied the President.

"It will be," concluded Anibal.

Toño's presence in opposition to the President had become unacceptable to the government, not so much for what he would say now, but for what he could say in the future. His articles criticized the government, but he was careful not to use any data stemming from his employment as a federal civil servant, even though it was difficult to not refer to projects and situations that had passed before him for budgetary approval.

His life had changed showing great improvement. He could head out late in the direction of the magazine, starting to work when he arrived. His responsibilities were fewer – editing and publishing the magazine – and so were his wages, but without major obligations the money earned was sufficient. The most important thing was the feeling of satisfaction he got from doing something that made him proud. He certainly could not have bought a feeling like this with his wages as a bureaucrat.

Ovidio, Manuel and Rogelio would still get together with Toño from time to time. They would talk about the many times they saw politicians doing political acrobatics, and they speculated about the future and what to expect. Toño did ask Manuel to stop meeting with them if he did not want to have problems with his job as a bureaucrat. Ovidio was added to his family's pharmaceutical business, which left him little time and lots of profits. Rogelio, however, had suffered the indignity of being rejected by a couple of multinational enterprises and was now offering, without much success, administrative and organizational consultations to private businesses. Toño was able to write several articles on the economy of Mexico, his name appearing in different publications, and he was appointed as a distinguished professor to the most important University in the country. His concerns were reflected in his written articles that referred mostly to the development of economic policy and the historical aspects of Mexican public finances. His writings could be harsh and boring to some extent, but there were always parts that were not only interesting but were applicable to current issues, and always prompted great discussions. The newspapers published in the capital followed his articles closely and always made public one or two of his comments, which aroused a great deal of interest.

In a previous article in *El Porvenir*, Toño had contested the widespread idea that the Mexican government had played an important role in the past in matters such as education and health. In that publication Toño had eloquently explained how the real social expenditures of the government were inadequate, taking into account the current circumstances, even though official statistics reported clearly put the government in a favorable light. The government reported that its social expenditures were 18.2% in 1940, decreasing slowly to 9.8% in 1952, to then increase gradually until it was 25.3% in 1972, finally collapsing to 8.1% in 1987, all these were indicated as percentages of the government's total expenditures budget. It was a very different story when the more orthodox and general method of reporting these data in terms of Gross Domestic Product (GDP) was used. To start, the percentages indicated in the budget were a very small part of the Gross Domestic Product: in 1972 the supposedly large amounts of 25.3% of the Expenditures Budget represented less than 4% of that year's GDP (approximately 30,780 millions). According to World Bank data the total social expenditure of the government of Mexico was less than 3% of the GDP from 1940 to 1960, and a little more than 3% from 1960 to 1976; in 1977 that amount completely collapsed, returning to an insignificant percentage. It was in 1981 that Mexican statistics for social expenditure reappeared, being 8.6% that year, followed by an average of 6.8% from 1982 to 1987, and 5.22% from 1989 to 2009 (when the average for Latin American expenditures overall was 12.9% in 1990-91, 14.9% in 1994-95, 15.9% in 2000-01 and 15.9% in 2005-06). It should be pointed out that public expenditures of the Mexican government included several items that were not a part of this category in other countries, expenses called "social development" that refer to the practically nonexistent actions against poverty, and to the cost of social safety and protection, which increased considerably after the year 2000.

In his article, Toño clearly explained that considering that growth through debt started in 1962 which allowed for an increase in social expenditures and represented a larger portion of the Budget, even in this era, social expenditure it still translated into a comparatively small amount in the final analysis if you consider that the Budget was not very big to start with. The costs of educating the farmers who had come to the city had increased to such an extent that the government was forced to provide this and other necessary services, which seemed to be the case if we look at the amounts allocated to educational expenditures. On the other hand, the article stated that, if the measures taken by the government through literacy programs, the survival of newborns, and medical services were greater in the cities, with difficulty could give itself the credit for being the only source of said increases in these areas. Other factors, like the expansion of private schooling and the provision of health insurance by non-public entities needed to also be taken into account.

It was clear that Toño's articles were more accusatory and revealing every time, and soon a sensational revelation was expected, which would force the government to deny it.

XXV

"For the wedge to tighten up it must be from the same wood"
Popular saying.

Without knowing what direction Toño would take, the inner circle quickly closed ranks. The President once again insisted that Anibal solve the problem that Toño and his publication represented, especially now that he was openly challenging the government.

"If you cannot solve the problem, I have many friends who can shut him up," said the President.

"Allow me to take care of it, please. He is someone I recommended and be assured that I can handle it," replied Anibal.

"Whatever is to be done must be accomplished today, before the next publication of the magazine," replied the President.

In the meantime, Toño worked feverishly on what would be the magazine's most important article in celebration of its third anniversary. His main argument was the evident failure of the Mexican regime with regard to social accomplishments that the country had suffered from the revolution to the present day. He argued that in 1962, the country continued to follow a cautious economic policy. A more populist approach was necessary, according to the President at that time, and although the policy of import substitution continued and a policy of moderate deficits was attempted, in the sixties it was decided that an expansionist policy was needed, but in the end the resulting inflation and debt servicing were too high for the revenue from oil to cover all expenditures.

The first part referred to the general policy of the country and would discuss import substitution, "stabilizing development", "shared development," and the success of other export economies compared to the Mexican disaster. Even though it seemed that the "Mexican miracle," the uninterrupted growth with little inflation and foreign debt from 1940 to 1962, was the correct economic policy, in truth it was not. This period mainly faced and, with a measure of success, the matter of growth, which ultimately resulted in the abandonment of the countryside and the emigration of a large portion of the rural population to the cities. This approach also deepened and widened the

91

disparity of income between the rural and urban populations and increased the existing inequality in Mexican society.

	Per Capita Average Quarterly Income **Rural** Areas Real Terms						
	1994	1996	1998	2000	2002	2004	Annual Average
Income from work	1,763	1063	1,548	1,969	1,979	2,238	1,760
Property rent	25	13	18	22	29	96	34
Private transfers	163	102	148	203	223	203	174
Public transfers	45	62	95	157	225	230	136
Other	17	15	12	11	15	1	12
Totals	2,012	1255	1,821	2,362	2,471	2,768	2,115

	Per Capita Average Quarterly Income **Urban** Areas Real Terms						
	1994	1996	1998	2000	2002	2004	Annual Average
Income from work	5,573	2,905	4,353	5,045	4,954	5,041	4,645
Property rent	100	70	112	100	109	132	104
Private transfers	279	178	247	219	178	266	228
Public transfers	214	119	259	329	299	352	262
Other	56	30	49	40	1	4	30
Totals	6,221	3,301	5,022	5,033	5,541	5795	5269

Sources: Agriculture Secretary, Rural Income Performance 1994-2004, April 2006, Tables I 4 & I 5.

The second part of the article concluded that in the beginning demographic growth had been stimulated by the Mexican government for a long time (until 1972), but then it was completely abandoned; however, the government's influence on reducing the fertility rate was considerable. Clearly the explosive demographic growth was due to the initial incentives given by the government, but even more importantly, these government policies resulted in the overcrowding and the struggle for survival we are now experiencing in the cities. Demographic growth has been finally reduced owing to, among other things, various government efforts and to the population itself, thanks to the many modern contraceptive measures available today; unfortunately, this decrease was forty years too late, resulting in many difficult challenges for the present and future of the country.

Although various topics were suggested, the main article in this issue of the magazine developed the idea that Mexico deserved to have been better governed.

Toño did consider the possible consequences of his articles, but it was vital that they be published. They would most than likely not attract much attention from those in the world of journalism, and though carefully written, they might pass unnoticed before the eyes of important bureaucrats, and above all, the general public. Although his personal safety and integrity might be in danger, he believed that an attack was an almost impossible option, especially if Anibal was, more than likely, still his friend.

The information to be shared with his readers in this issue was important, and it had not been published before. *El Porvenir* and Toño did not pretend to compete with the many government spokesmen, who surely were already preparing their contributions extolling the government's accomplishments. But Toño had written his articles in such a way that it was very difficult to disagree with him. For example, the pro-birth position of President Echeverria at the beginning of his term was well known and appeared in several of his public statements; however, when he later changed his mind issued the Law of Population in 1972 and set up the National Council of Population, which it was discovered was never able to move beyond the investigative phase, in spite of praise from journalists paid by the government.

Taking into consideration his criticism as well as what the government and its supporters had said regarding this topic, Toño felt that he should inform the government bureaucracy about the article before its publication and that he should ask for any appropriate comments in case there were any errors or seemingly incorrect observations. With this in mind, he called his friend Aníbal, who was out of the office. He would wait for his call back before publishing the article, as long as answered within a reasonable period of time. But the amount of time he was willing to wait for him to answer took longer than expected, so he went ahead and ordered the printing of his article and then, using the traditional back window as a shortcut, left to eat something in the food stands located behind the building.

It was common practice, up to a point, to leave through a window from the back of the building to buy food, thereby saving time; furthermore, it would appear as if no one had not actually left the building, an advantage that was used by most of the employees. That night, almost all the workers had already left the building assuming that the next issue of *El Porvenir* was ready to be printed, but for the final edit of Toño's article. Finally, after having spent plenty of time rereading the written text, the article was ready and he felt like a great weight had finally been lifted off of him. Francisco, the longstanding editor of *El Porvenir*, asked Toño to leave the final draft of his article for him to proofread before leaving to get some food.

The night was humid and although the temperature had already dropped, soon it would start to fall even more. Surely, once sunrise arrived, the sun would start to shine and once more would fill every space with faint light and abundant heat. Toño felt that the time had come to begin to use certain precautions, especially now that his articles started to gloss over the regime's "great achievements." Perhaps he should start sending his articles by messenger and should consider changing his residence. He had not noticed anyone watching him, but surely someone from the state security forces was following him.

In the meantime, Francisco, in the offices of *El Porvenir*, was engaged in the task of giving Toño's article a final review. His devotion to the magazine was most evident, and he looked at each issue as if it were his own writing. This article in particular was surely going to be carefully reviewed by the local press and should therefore appear in perfect text.

Francisco was proofreading the last lines when two armed men barged in the editing room, kicking the entrance door violently, which was not locked, and without saying a word fired into the area where Francisco was working, wounding him fatally. Without stopping to confirm the outcome of this atrocity, they threatened two employees still in the printing area, who were standing next to the large linotypes, and asked for Toño, using, strangely, a name he never used: Antonio Morales Muñoz.

XXVI

"Fear does not ride a donkey"
Popular saying.

It was the Day of the Death. Excited people hurried home, some to finish their offerings for those who had departed to the other world before them, others simply to rest from an exhausting workday. Most, however, were in the churches or in the cemeteries to honor their ancestors, whose memory was still fresh in the minds of the living.

Toño did not share their hustle, not that he did not remember Don Gabriel and others with affection, but today he had to print a special article before the deadline about the government's actions to be included in the last edition to be published with tomorrow's date. His brief departure from the office seemed unnecessary, however, he planned to bring back something to eat for his colleagues who had stayed after work to make sure the publication went out on time. It comes with the job, he thought. His unnoticed departure, which surely the professional killers waiting to assassinate him had ignored when they mounted surveillance and entered the magazine's offices, had saved his life, but had cost the life of Francisco, his editor, who had still been working on Toño's article. Upon Toño's return, he encountered much confusion, but he soon realized that an order had been issued to assassinate him, which had turned out to be disastrous, in spite of his own good luck.

The murder of a journalist in a country like Mexico is a common ocurrence, but an assassination order issued by the President of the country is rare and could almost be considered an honor. It was obvious that his friend Anibal had decided to join the side of the winners. It was crucial that he immediately warn his closest friends, hoping it was not too late. He was elated when he was able to reach Rogelio to tell him what had happened. Both Rogelio and Ovidio should take the events seriously and should take flight. Toño did not want to know where. It was best that he did not know.

It was vital for Toño to disappear for a while, and although the Mexican security system could be circumvented, the one implemented by the American Central Intelligence Agency, CIA, would be almost impossible to escape, Toño thought. The only reason for the government of the United States of America

95

not to look for him when requested to do so by the Mexican government, would be if the information sought after was as valuable to them as it was to the Mexican government, and fortunately it was.

The most important thing to do after escaping was to find a good hiding place, even before taking the next step. The one impossible place for the security forces to find him was in the outskirts of the city with a close relative of a trusted friend who was above all suspicion. The secret police would not be able to locate him there, in the middle of a collection of huts that was unfamiliar to them.

That November second Toño felt more lonsome than ever: his friends had fled in unknown directions and he could not go home. His only refuge was Rachel, his long-time lover. Before departing for his hiding place, he asked her to meet him at the house of a mutual friend, and soon they met up with the same familiarity and urgency as with someone who was already family. After telling her what had happened, Toño then realized that it would have been better if she had not known anything, but it was too late to protect her. Their conversation was long and difficult, but in the end common sense prevailed and they both agreed that it was best to go to the American security people to request safe-conduct. There was an element of risk, but it was his best option at this point. Rachel should flee as well, but she refused to, indicating that she could always argue that she had not seen him. Toño felt that her argument was weak and he would have preferred that she escape while it was still possible. But to convince a stubborn woman was not just difficult, it was impossible.

Trying to establish contact with the Americans was not easy, especially under the scrutiny of the Mexican agents. Toño did not want to use Rachel under any circumstance, so the doubtful honor fell on Hector, Toño's favorite janitor at the government office where he had been an audit underminister. The main purpose was to let an American security agent know that someone with important information was willing to give it to them in exchange for their protection and the approval of an application for asylum. The source of the information, an ex-member of the Mexican federal government's economic team, guaranteed that the information had not been previously revealed and that the government of the United States of America could use it in whatever way it best suited them.

The negotiations were delayed because the American government wanted additional information before committing to anything. Toño had to agree to reveal that direct foreign investment last year was lower than the official government numbers, especially the direct foreign investment coming from the United States of America. This allowed the negotiations to move forward to the point that they agreed to relocate him to an American city on the border. He was told to go to a shopping center in the city, from where he would be picked up and protected under diplomatic immunity until arriving at the border, where he would be met by security agents who would then interrogate him.

Waiting at the shopping center had been agonizing, but after a short while the American agents identified themselves and took him in a car with diplomatic plates to a secluded section of an airport where a private plane was waiting to take him to an unspecified American border city. The trip was long and boring and the city where they landed unrecognizable. There was no doubt it was a city

in the United States of America: the American flag was waving everywhere and in the distance you could see a collection of unmistakably American fast-food restaurants. Toño was even less uncertain when, after disembarking from the airplane, he was asked to go to a huge room where there was a very large table around which more than fifteen people who did not speak Spanish were anxiously waiting to hear his secrets.

At first, Toño felt intimidated by the many participants, but soon he felt comfortable with them and with the procedure they followed. The questions were frequent and intense, and followed a chronological order. Initially the topics were carefully selected by the questions posed by the representatives of each of the participating groups. Later, when Toño was no longer willing to continue answering questions, the questions ended.

The first questions were regarding the particulars of the presidential transactions, to which Toño was able to reply in detail. Later questions asked about issues regarding the balance of payments, imports, exports and illegal transactions by politicians in particular. The many participants would write every question and corresponding answer in their notebooks. Toño refused to answer questions not directly related to illegal transfers of money overseas by Mexican politicians.

The information that Toño had shared became of public domain when he decided, on his own, to publish it in an American newspaper and in the magazine *El Porvenir*. What Toño wrote appeared in its entirety in the local newspaper, without causing a stir, neither in the village of his residence abroad, nor in the capital of the Mexican country where he was well known. What was sent to the Mexican magazine was never published, surely because the editors of *El Porvenir* were afraid the magazine would be closed down, or perhaps because it never arrived into the hands of its editors. Furthermore, what was written in the border town newspaper did not have a major impact, nor was it reproduced in any other more important publications. The United States of America press, you could say, had remained silent, to the benefit of the Mexican government, which was unusual though not entirely impossible.

With the passing of time his secrets were losing value and later events would marginalized them. The main protagonists would change, but not what Toño had said, nor the consequences resulting from his words. Apparently, the danger his words represented was never lost, and although he relied on the fact that his revelation had lost some strength, his treason would not be forgiven, either then or later.

XXVII

"Only when the nopal cactus has prickly pears do we notice it"
Popular saying.

Toño thought about Rachel constantly, he wanted her to come and meet up with him. He dreamed of an encounter, yet he could not do much to make it happen. He must maintain his silence to protect her and he must remain in exile to escape the execution order. After a time without anyone having heard from him, not even his family, Rachel thought that Toño was perhaps dead. In any case, disappeared or dead, it meant the same to her: there was no one to wait for. The one thing she was left with was her loyal friend Gregorio, who had always been willing to wait for her, even knowing that was Toño who she preferred.

On a day like any other, Rachel, now 39 years old, decided not to wait any longer and married Gregorio without conditions, with the understanding that Toño, whether dead or not, was dead to her. Toño never expected so great a betrayal, but his heart was unmoved when he heard what Rachel had done. He did not even attempt to send a message; time and distance had destroyed everything.

The days passed, and little by little so did the years. The Mexican politicians boldly displayed their ill-gotten luxuries, and frequently showed up abroad, flaunting their money. Toño was able to start a swimming pool maintenance business, on which he spent all his time and from which he made sufficient money to live comfortably in his new country. Unexpectedly, one autumn afternoon someone he knew, who he had not seen in a long time, crossed the threshold of his office, sat on his new sofa and asked him for a favor that would be difficult to grant. It was one of the diplomats who had brought him to this country and he asked to help him negotiate the terms of a loan involving millions of dollars with the Mexican government, now represented by a new President, along with several Ministers. At first Toño wanted absolutely nothing to do with this favor, above all because it might involve people he knew. However, as he listened, he began to realize that the request could turn into an order to which he was vulnerable, especially, he feared, because he had no political support in this country. The speaker told a good story, but it was clear that the welcoming mat could be withdrawn if Toño rejected what appeared to be but a consultation. In the end, he agreed to do it, with the one condition that he not be physically present at the negotiations. He could be in an adjacent room or available to talk by phone, but he would not be in the presence of the Mexican negotiators.

The date of the meeting soon arrived, and arrangements for Toño to participate from afar were made. The negotiations were important for both the Mexicans and the officials of the United States of America, his new country. This very large loan to be granted by the American government should help to stabilize the exaggerated expense of the Mexican government. The part that Toño was consulted on referred to the guarantee that the loan would fund specific projects, without allowing any moneys to fall into the hands of the ambitious Mexican politicians. Toño did not not know any of the President's companions or counselors except for Anibal, his friend when he had been a member of the Mexican government. The negotiations took place in a slow and orderly fashion, and the Americans delivered on their word, giving Toño an adjoining room from where he could see and hear every detail of the talks.

From time-to-time, various advisors would come to consult with him about some detail. They especially wanted to know what the Mexican negotiators would decide when a point was reached that required a decision. Toño was in deep trouble because his allegiance, although clearly for the Americans, at times could not be against the Mexicans. The negotiations were not evenly balanced, as they have never been between these two countries, and Toño's tendency was to lean in favor of the Mexicans which were the weaker group. On the other hand, the Mexicans had tried to kill him and he had no sympathy for them. The best would have been to not be in such a position. Regardless, the objective was to try to make the best out of a difficult situation. As usual, the Mexican group ended up accepting unacceptable terms, and the protective measures for the funds were agreed upon by all.

Even though he was invited to the social gathering at the end of the negotiations, he preferred not to attend then or at any other time. For this reason he was greatly surprised to receive a phone call from Anibal inviting him for dinner the following day. Without any pretensions of being a diplomat, Toño got together with his old friend in an elegant restaurant near Anibal's hotel. Their conversation began as a recrimination, and without noticing, they both behaved distantly, as if they already were what they now were, two strangers with very different ideas about what should be done.

"I never thought you would commit treason against me, and as you see I live here thanks to your machinations," said Toño.

"I always thought you would see it that way and that is why I have asked you to meet with me. I did not commit treason against you, on the contrary, it was thanks to my interventions that you were able to get away and that Rachel was not tortured," said Anibal somberly.

"How can that be true, you are a corrupt politician, you always have been," added Toño.

"That attribute is insulting and I really do not deserve it, especially from someone like you," replied Anibal, who continued,

"Let me tell you, you have always been an idealist confused about what is correct and what is not. You have always followed ideals that do not exist. Now that you are facing reality, you still do not see it. I am the one who always was, someone important, with money and friends, you are nothing," he added.

Toño started to get up from his chair with the clear intention of leaving the place.

"Wait, sit down again. We shouldn't insult each other, I have always had a fondness for you, and in spite of everything I still retain some of that," stated Anibal moving his arm in a clear signal.

"Nevertheless, I myself have no fondness for you," replied Toño, sitting down again, but without sitting in the chair properly.

"I understand your feelings, but there are things that need to be said between you and me," asserted Anibal

"To start, there is the question of reality, which you have never understood. We live only once, and all our efforts should be concentrated on our achievements and, as you can see, I have achieved a lot. You, on the other hand, have wasted everything because ideas that cannot become reality because they are just that, only ideas," affirmed Anibal. "To compensate yourself enough, even if having to ignore traditional rules, is what is expected of an efficient, important public official. To accept the corruption of one's colleagues means to join in their deceptions but also to be a part of an enterprise made up of a small group of people that are aware of what surrounds them. It is a group that cannot be reproached by their families for being poor or mediocre, because they will never be." continued saying Anibal.

"But the price you have to pay for corruption is too high, you will always be someone labelled as a corrupt politician, even if you claim as yours the millions stolen from the people," replied Toño.

"Nevertheless, look at us now: I am a guest of honor in a foreign country surrounded by good wishes and treated like royalty, and you are an outcast who can barely pay basic necessities to survive. That is the difference between idealism and realism in politics," indicated Anibal triumphantly.

"What will make a difference is the future, the one inherited by your children and your country. They will always remember you as a corrupt person who supported the powerful and hid in their shadows to take advantage of the weak and to rob the public treasury," Toño finally said.

"You should know that my children are aware of my exploits in politics and they are proud that they have enough to be able to freely choose their own path and to readily have access to everything they could need," concluded Anibal.

"Part of the problem is that you are never going to be able to tell the difference between what is good and what is corrupt because for you everything is the same," indicated Toño with exasperation.

"Wrong again, a government can be so big and complex that to manage it requires an intelligent and knowledgeable group of people who cannot be supervised by a President alone. For example, Mexico's society has reached a size and complexity that is difficult to administer. The Presidents have been grateful that some assistants have successfully controlled part of the complex totality," affirmed Anibal.

XXVIII

"These are not enchiladas to be made!"
Popular saying.

"But how do you explain the clearly unacceptable, even unethical management of policy in place during the presidency of Gustavo Diaz Ordaz as well as those in place during the six-term term periods of Luis Echeverria, Jose Lopez Portillo and Carlos Salinas de Gortari?" Toño stressed.

"You cannot include the period under Gustavo Diaz Ordaz, when Antonio Ortiz Mena was Minister of Finance since he achieved the best growth record without inflation in the history of Mexico," Anibal said.

"Ja! That is precisely the lie the regime you belong to has been telling: that this was the most brilliant period in the recent history of the country. This is simply not true. Antonio Ortiz Mena was always a very capable manager, as he demonstrated while leading the Mexican Institute of Social Security (IMSS), the Interamerican Bank (BID) and the Mexican Ministry of Finance. However, his management of the government's economy was always subject to the directives of his political bosses, and he never dared to implement urgently needed changes during his time with the Mexican government. Politicians like you idolize him, but it is time to face reality," Toño put forth, taking the initiative and fully occupying his seat.

"What I came to tell you is that you are against history. Modern countries are formed when a solid government is fully organized, generally with a strong man in command. Mexico has not been the exception. Bureaucrats like myself are merely subordinates of a greater enterprise which benefits many people. The "theft" you referred to is but a small contribution for the great sacrifice that all of us have made in knowledge, experience and personal effort. Without our contribution the country would fall into chaos and mediocrity," Anibal said with conviction.

"It is interesting how you see yourself now, but your mask conceals a vulgar thief and an accomplice to all manner of outrages you have had to cover up. Tell me if a wrong decision made by a President does not decide the future of a newborn whose mother has gone for help to a clinic for the poor, only to find out that it has been closed," Toño pointed out raising his voice.

103

"I have no illusions, you do what you can, and in Mexico you cannot do very much. Each of our Presidents have made a major attempt to improve the economy. For example, José López Portillo was a man who, despite everything, secured benefits for everybody and fought against greed as well," replied Anibal.

"No one can say that Jose Lopez Portillo was not a great person when he became President, but he was a very different person at that time from the diminished and beaten man who finished destroying the national economy by the end of his presidency. Surely almost all the Presidents started with good intentions, but ended up beaten and frustrated," replied Toño.

"That is precisely the sacrifice I am talking about. To work for the government, you know, is not easy when you have a position of responsibility. You must suffer many humiliations and, sometimes, you live literally saying "Jesus" since someone can have you fired at any moment. It is most definitely not an easy thing to be an important bureaucrat," concluded Anibal.

"What are you going to tell me about the complicity in the bribes and the assassinations ordered by your bosses? Is it also compensated by your stealing? affirmed Toño, angrily.

"That version is of your own creation, and is one held by idealists like you. Even if it could be confirmed, It is a small price to pay for the progress of the country. If you want to build a country you more than likely have to control those people unable to see your purpose" Anibal declared. "All societies need a government and all modern governments must lead societies in accordance with their political objectives. In the case of Mexico, the government has provided leadership and a modern administration. You cannot ask for more," completed Anibal.

"Let me tell you that in the first place I do not believe that every society needs a government, it needs leadership, and that you can get from a group who do not accept corruption and who hold honesty and efficiency as principal directive. In the second place, a majority of governments do seem to profess that honesty and transparency direct their objectives. When the government is a group of unscrupulous men, like it was Mexico during most of the period under the PRI, the people should reject them, which is happening now. A corrupt and criminal government has no future anywhere. Frankly, I do not see things like you do. For me, honesty is the most important virtue because only under its influence can one build a strong country on a solid foundation; otherwise, the history of corruption will continue thereby impeding the successful development of the country. You can see that in the history of Mexico," Toño said.

"I am not going to discuss something as trivial as the historic record. But let me ask you, how else would it be possible for Mexico to reach a level of development comparable to that of developed countries?" replied Anibal.

"I believe that Mexico will never be developed in the same terms than the so-called first world countries. Mexico, despite its need for universal standards, will in the long run adopt some, perhaps many, but it will keep certain elements that identify it as a country, such as those related to the sun, the belief in something intangible and the attachment to the collective. The original peoples are still with us, and they probably will always be," completed Toño looking directly into Anibal's eyes.

There was no more to say between these two who had long been friends. Anibal was a Mexican of the past, from those who preferred to advance themselves without considering others, the new Mexican society would have to destroy these beliefs if it was to move forward towards a better future, thought Toño, getting up and offering to pay for the food that he had hardly touched.

"No, I will pay the bill, after all, courtesy is a tradition of the Mexican people," affirmed Anibal, who suddenly appeared tired and haggard to Toño's eyes.

"Thank you for everything and *provecho*," said Toño without knowing what more to say.

That would be the last time he would see Anibal.

XXIX

"When in a foreign land follow suit"
Popular saying.

Not long after the negotiations, Toño realized that he could still be vulnerable with regard to the American government, so he started to plan a new escape, and this time he would make sure to completely disappear not only from the Mexican government but the American government as well, his new hiding place would be in Canada. Toño wondered, upon arriving in this new country, whether he would encounter a different world. He had yet to experience the difference between the southern and northern regions of North America. He would soon discover that they were two very different developed worlds.

His first impression was that he was in the presence of a totally different way of life to what he had known up until now. Although forty five years of age already, he felt totally renewed. Society was rich and had everything one could need. The economy and the politics were perfectly managed and coordinated. The government, which was socialist, administered the programs that benefited the people, and monitored economic performance, mostly private, which was free to act in matters related to business. Personal initiative was stimulated and all major decisions were made by freely elected politicians. Perhaps the most important thing Toño noticed was the concept of self-sufficiency, and the idea that each one person is an independent individual worthy of being taken into account.

The most important characteristic, he thought, was the concept of equality. There were few social strata, and he often would see examples of behavior that made him remember, with sadness, the place from where he had originally come from. No one here would treat him as if he could not pay, or as if he was not a person. Everyone, absolutely everyone, would respect him even without knowing who he was or where he came from.

There were certainly many differences, but one of the most incredible was the respect for the law and for the rights of the individuals. This has been cultivated to the point that even in winter you could trust that every car would stop when you crossed a street with a pedestrian crosswalk in the middle of it. And of course, there was the concept of solidarity. He now understood what to defend human rights really meant, in fact, he now fully comprehended what human rights truly were, which had been an abstract idea before, but was now something he could embrace whole-heartedly, thinking nostalgically about the city he had come from.

The winter cold and snow were something new to which he would have to adapt. Coming from a warm place, he was wondering if he could do it as he walked along on one of the main streets of the city, and turned from a narrow single lane street to a wider street with several lanes going up what was the only hill in the entire city. It was snowing copiously, but he was well covered with his brand-new worsted yarn cap, his flannel scarf and a new immigrant coat, bought without shame, in the most popular store for new immigrants with little money. All of a sudden, surprisingly, the car at the top of the hill started to spin out of control and stopped before reaching the top. The moment was, Toño realized, a dangerous one. When, suddenly and with no prior notice, the drivers of the other vehicles that were starting to climb the hill moved their cars perpendicularly, to keep them from sliding down the hill, and got out, all of them, and rushing towards the vehicle in trouble, started to push it up the hill until it reached the top and disappeared on its way down the other side. No one cursed the driver in trouble, and no one congratulated anyone for their good deed. Everyone simply went back to their cars and drove off as if nothing had happened.

This was not the only time this new culture amazed him. To get to his school to improve his new language, Toño had to take the city bus that passed on the street in front of his apartment. Everything seemed so desolate during winter, which lasted more than six months; it seemed implausible that the urban bus would arrive at the solitary stop near his apartment on time and that someone would actually be waiting for it. It was a considerable distance from his building to the bus stop, especially when the ground was covered in snow and the wind was blowing steadily. And yet, Toño had learned that the urban bus would be there at the time indicated on the schedule attached to the lonely pole marking the bus stop. The social organization was stronger than anything, even stronger than winter.

A major key tenet among modern Canadian politicians was that they should respect the principles of honesty and transparency, and that if they did not it would automatically disqualify them from public life. Almost no one was willing to cheat or to take advantage of others. After all, he said to himself, this was a first world country.

Although perfect in so many ways, the social system had yet to find a definitive remedy for the drug addicts and the homeless living on the streets who had decided to not participate in a consumer society. It also did not seem to have found an acceptable answer for the indigenous population, which had a lower economic level and whose culture had not been fully integrated into the general culture. The lack of solutions to these problems created the future agenda of this advanced country, offering a series of passionately debated proposals which, it is thought, would resolve some of these problems.

Toño thought of calling Rachel, but she had not shown any special interest in this new country of his, far from the corrupted politics that had exiled him. He did want to make sure Rachel had not experienced any problems with his disappearance. Apparently her declaration of not having seen him had satisfied the Mexican security agents. It was likely that she would be under surveillance for some time, but perhaps his lack of communication, the intervention of American Central Intelligence Agency agents, or even Anibal's intercession on her behalf, had protected her from being harassed or even tortured. Her marriage to Gregorio had destroyed him emotionally and he would have liked to tell her what he thought of her betrayal. It was too late for any reaction, however, and the best thing to do at this point was to let her know that he only wished her happiness, which he always had.

What satisfied Toño was to live in a society where the great principles he had studied came alive and were put into practice. Human rights not only existed, but life was respected, in contrast to what would happen in Mexico. If someone died either accidentally or intentionally, the person responsible, no matter who he or she was, would be punished. He had finally arrived at a place where the rules he had studied existed, were in effect, and were important.

XXX

"Life is worth nothing"
Popular song.

His great knowledge of governmental economy and his experience in the anteroom of government seemed lost forever. It was for this reason that he decided, more than fourteen years later, to publish a series of articles about his experience during the time he spent working in the government of Mexico. He was unexpectedly surprised when his words appeared in the pages of *El Porvenir*, which had barely survived, and became a topic of conversation among present-day politicians. Even the local newspaper in Canada printed part of the text, making him a celebrity, at least for a couple of weeks. His brief encounter with the past soon ended, without any outstanding events, and his life returned to normal.

His former colleagues had embarked on different lives, unrelated to their former interests. Rogelio was now the successful manager of one of the larger banks in the country. His subservience to the bank's commercial policies was absolute, and he never thought about the fraud Toño had uncovered, and, of course, he never mentioned it to anyone. As for Ovidio, his life was more difficult but well-paid, having been reduced to the role of salesman and having had to remain in hiding for a long time. Eventually, the family business gave him the opportunity to form part of the management team. He always wondered whether his past continued to work against him.

Anibal, Toño's former close friend, became part of the team of the next President, having been recommended by the former one, and before long he filled his pockets with the people's money, retiring abroad in a safe and quiet place in Spain. Everything was apparently over. Manuel having kept Toño's secret, drifted through several government departments until finally, without any political sponsorship, he ended up returning abroad where he could trade his knowledge for a good salary.

It was then that Toño, feeling that his past was safely behind him, decided to visit his family, some of his friends, and especially Rachel, who he had abandoned when he decided to leave the country. Rachel had never understood why she was left behind. At that time, Toño had thought it would be easier to protect her by freeing her from any connection to him. He had thought he would ask her to join him or that he would go and find her after some time had gone by. But nothing ever materialized. Time passed and the daily hassles of life made Toño forget his promises. In the end Rachel married Gregorio and had the family she always had wanted. Although she continued to think about Toño, she believed he would never come back, she believed he was dead.

Toño arrived in Mexico City in early November, encountering a very different city from the one he had left. No one was there to receive him when he arrived. Each street seemed unrecognizable and new, as they crossed them in the old taxi, even when they finally arrived at his hotel. The city had changed completely, it was full of people, and the weather was unfamiliar. The afternoon was grey and the city was enveloped by a permanent cloud of pollution, surely due to the many vehicles endlessly meandering along every street as far as you could see. The afternoon had become cloudy, and you could smell rain in the air. Tomorrow he would get to see Rachel and his family. Toño had resigned himself a long time ago to wishing her the happiness he could not, or did not want to, give her. In a certain way, he was happy for her good luck and wished her a happy life.

Today, Day of the Dead, was a day for reflection, and Toño decided to leave his hotel room and roam the streets of the city. The sad outcome of a popular revolution still moved him, and although he no longer felt a part of that history, he continued to ask himself if there could have been a different outcome to the social conflict that would have allowed Mexicans to access modernity. If only the winners of that bloody struggle had not been Obregon and Calles, surely the development of the country would have been different, perhaps better, perhaps worse, a possible future that will never be known.

The tragedy that had resulted was of immeasurable and historic proportions. The subsequent governments, led and defined by its Presidents, learned to lie and exaggerate when it would have been easier simply to learn about economics. They lied and exaggerated to the people and to themselves by pointing out the achievements of a monopolistic and authoritarian administration. Every contributor to those lies, knowing the truth was guilty of defrauding the populace, which have always struggled between life and death.

He slowly walked along the sidewalk leading to the nearest forest, reflecting on these old topics, he noticed how a lot of people hurried up to escape the imminent rain, although the multitude was such that the people seemed to never end. Finally, when the rain began to fall, the crowd started to slowly thin out as the majority of the people sought shelter in the buildings along the avenue. But Toño continued to calmly walk towards the space full of trees and grass that attracted him in the distance. It was then that two assassins, dressed in gabardines and waiving their automatic weapons jumped out of an indistinguishable car and approached Toño, shooting him almost point blank. His body fell to the sidewalk, before reaching the green space, and while his attackers returned to the vehicle they had exited from, Toño felt for the last time the tiny drops of water hitting his face. He was forty nine years old.

Rachel and her family never met Toño.

The attack was never reported, and no mention of it appeared in any newspaper, neither local nor foreign. The country's leaders had eliminated a subversive and dangerous traitor, someone who had attempted to destroy the most important norms and rules that wove together the fabric of the country. The groups in power could be now at peace, there was no one to leak any information to anyone, anymore. Everything was under control.

SUPPLEMENTAL STATISTICAL APPENDIX
I – National Economic Data

	Annual Average Growth Rate %			
	1950-62	1963-70	1971-81	1982-94
Gross Domestic Product (GDP)	6.1	7.0	6.9	1.7
Economically Active Population	2.9	1.7	4.1	3.6
Debt Servicing	1.2	2.3	3.3	5.5

Source: Enrique Cárdenas. La Política Económica en México 1950-1994, Chart VI-I. p. 62

	GDP[a]		Annual inflation[b]	Foreign debt[c]		Actual Exchange rate[d]	Official Exchange rate[d]
	US Dlrs[f]	%	%	% GDP	US Mill.	$/Dlr	$/Dlr.
1950	11.84[e]	9.72	11.0[e]	0.08	912.0		8.65
1960	13.04	4.000	4.84[e]	4.63	603.7		12.50
1970	35.52	6.502	4.69	17.05	6,056.1	27.2	12.50
1980	194.3	9.233	29.85	31.41	61,029.6	19.7	22.95
1990	262.7	5.176	29.93	53.52	140,597.0	25.8	2,838.37
2000	707.9	4.942	8.96	41.85	296,256.1		9.45
2010	1,058	5.118	4.40	42.23	446,793.4		12.38
2015	1,170	3.288	2.13	54.03	632,151.0		17.33

Sources: [a]Mexico maxico, Economía Mexicana, México 2010 & Julio 2018. [f]$US current prices. [b]Worl Bank. BIRF, AIF, Data, México GDP. [b]World Wide Inflation, Inflation.eu, Historic Inflation Mexico, Consumer Price Index (CPI) Inflation, 2010-2020. [c]Enrique Cárdenas, La Política Económica en Mexico 1950-1994, Appendix A-4 Indicadores Macroeconómicos p. 214. [d]Enrique Cárdenas. La Política Económica en México 1950-1994, p. 69.

	GDP[a] (thousand Pesos)	Population[b] (millions)	Homicides drug trade[c] (million)	Expense corruption[d]	Support expense Army[d]
2007	1,053,000	109,170,502	2,826	--	--
2008	1,110,000	110,815,271	6,837	6,400	65,000
2009	900,045	112,463,887	11,753	--	76,000

2010	1,058,000	114,092,963	19,546	5,950	80,000
2011	1,180,000	115,695,473	24,068	5,000	96,050
2012	1,201,000	117,274,155	18,161	4,200	84,000
2014	1,315,000	120,355,128	--	5,900	96,000
2015	1,171,000	121,858,258	--	6,100	105,000
2016	1,078,000	123,333,376	--	6,050	98,000
2018	1,221,000	126,190,788	--	5,650	97,000

Sources: [a]World Bank, BIRD, AID, Data México GDP. [b]World Bank, BIRD, AID, Data México Population. [c]Jhonatan D. Rosen & Roberto Zepeda M. Revista Reflexiones, La Guerra contra el Narcotráfico en México, 2015, Vol. 94 No. 1, p. 163. [d]Centro de Investigación Económica y Presupuestaria (CIEP), Gasto Público en Seguridad, Una mirada a la ruta de los recursos pp. 78 & 91 (Data about expenditures on corruption and army assistance are taken from Graph on pages 78 and 91).

Public and Private Savings - Mexico 2001-2010

	2001	2002	2003	2004	2005	2006	2007	2008	2009	2010
Private	17.8	16.7	16.2	14.6	15.8	18.1	18.6	17.7	16.3	15.3
Public	3.4	3.2	2.7	2.6	1.0	0.9	1.1	1.8	2.7	3.2

Source: J Tapia Maruri, Evolución Reciente y Perspectivas de la Economía Mexicana 2000-2010, Comercio Exterior Vol 62, No.6, Nov & Dic 2012, p. 27

Foreign Debt of México as GDP percentage (1915-2015)

1915	11.16	1950	0.08	1985	56.80
1920	14.73	1960	4.63	1990	53.52
1930	24.55	1970	17.05	2000	41.85
1940	21.67	1980	31.41	2015	54.03

Source: International Monetary Fund. Country economy. com

Annual Inflation of México as a GDP percentage (1970-2018)

1970	4.69	1990	29.93	2010	4.40
1975	11.31	1995	51.97	2015	2.13
1980	29.85	2000	8.96	2018	4.83
1985	63.75	2005	3.33		

Fuente: Worldwide Inflation Data. en Inflation.eu

Financing of the Economy 1970-1982 (% GDP)

	1970-75	1976-81	1982
Total Investment	20.3	21.8	21.1
External savings	3.4	4.4	3.5
Internal savings	16.9	17.4	17.6

113

Private savings			
Private investment	13.2	12.6	11.8
Private savings	15.7	17.0	25.0
Balance	2.5	4.4	13.2
Public sector			
Public investment	7.1	9.2	9.3
Public savings	1.2	0.4	-7.6
Balance	-5.9	-8.8	-16.9

Source: Enrique Cárdenas. La Política Económica en México 1950-1994, Chart III. 4. p. 102

Sector Contribution to the Growth of GDP 1950-1958

(Pesos 1960 %)	1950-58	Tasa Annual
Agriculture	15.3	5.5
Industry	25.8	7.7
Services	29.2	6.2

Source: Enrique Cárdenas. La Hacienda Pública y la Política Económica 1929 -1958, Cuadro V. 3 p. 142

Sector Contribution to the Growth of GDP 1962-1971
(pesos 1960 %)

	1962	1971	Tasa Anual
Agriculture	15.3	11.5	3.7
Industry	29.6	34.1	8.9
Services	56.2	55.6	7.0

Source: Enrique Cárdenas. La Política Económica en México 1950-1994, Cuadro II. 1 p. 60

Internal Demand   External Demand   Import substitutions
1940-1945

	Internal Demand	External Demand	Import Substitution
1940-1945			
Todas las Industrias	29.6	78.9	-8.6
1945-1950			
Todas las Industrias	130.2	54.0	25.5

Source: Indicadores Macroeconómicos en Enrique Cárdenas, La Política Económica en México 1950-1994, Chart VI-I, p. 62

114

II – Income Distribution

	Salary income & Non Salary income Agriculture sector & non-agriculture sector %[c]					
	1989	1990	1991	1992	1993	1994
Agrarian Sector						
Salary Income	-4.2	-8.8	-0.1	-2.8	0.1	0.1
Non Salary Income	10.9	11.2	0.3	-10.0	-4.5	-4.4
Non Agrarian Sector						
Salary Income	9.8	7.1	9.8	9.8	7.7	7.7
Non Salary Income	9.9	5.4	2.3	0.0	-0.3	5.7
Rate of Real Change	83.6	83.2	91.2	96.9	103.2	97.2

Source: Based on data from [a]Macrotrends, Mexico Urban Population 1960-2020. [b]Percentage of total population. [c]N. Lustig & M. Székely México Evolución Económica, Pobreza y Desigualdad, Table 8 p. 31.

GINI

1950	1958	1963	1968	1977	1989	1994	1996
0.520[a]	0.530[a]	0.606[b]	0.586[b]	0.482[b]	0.543[c]	0.543[c]	0.548[c]
0.512[b]	0.451[b]	0.530[b]	0.540[a]	0.496[e]	0.542[f]	0.491[f]	0.470[f]
0.504[g]	0.518[g]	0.584[h]	0.498[e]	0.524[i]	0.480[j]	0.548[k]	0.528[k]

1998	2000	2002	2004	2005	2006	2008	2010	2015	2016
0.534	0.526	0.465[l]	0.469[l]	0.471[m]	0.459[l]	0.470[l]	0.446[l]	0.452[l]	0.463[c]
0.469	0.493	0.479[n]	0.469[o]	0.487[p]	0.481[q]	0.482[q]	0.471[q]	0.492[n]	0.448[r]
0.544	0.539	0.443[s]	0.466[s]	0.466[s]	0.448[s]	0.470[c]	0.469[r]	0.468[t]	0.498[u]

Sources: [a]Lustig & Székely in International Monetary Fund, Corbacho & Schwartz Working Paper WP 02/12, p. 8. [b]O. Altimir in Distribución del Ingreso en México Ensayos (Banxico) Vol. III O. Gomez & E. Arnaud, La Política Presupuestaria del Sector Público y su Incidencia en la Distribución del Ingreso, Chart 4, p. 49 [c]Federal Reserve Bank of Saint Louis (FRED), Economic Datos, GINI para Mexico. [d]World Bank, IBRD, AID, Data. Mexico, GINI. [e]F. Cortés, Medio Siglo de Desigualdad en Mexico, March 2013, Graph 1, p. 14. [f]F. Cortés y D. Vargas La Evolución de la Desigualdad en México: Viejos y Nuevos Resultados, Graph 3, p. 49. [g]A. García Rocha, La Desigualdad Económica en México, El Colegio de México, 1986, p. 146. [h]Bergman (1981) in O. Gomez & E. Arnaud Distribución del Ingreso de México, Vol. I, Chart p. 69. [i]Desarrollo Humano y Desigualdad en México, Graph 1, Universidad de Guadalajara. [j]M Székely in International Monetary Fund, Corbacho & Schwartz Working Paper WP 02/12, p. 8. [k]R. Campos, G. Esquivel & N. Lustig, The Rise and Fall of Inequality in México 1989-2010. Table A.1. [l]F. Cortés & D. Vargas La Evolución de la Desigualdad en México: Viejos y Nuevos Resultados, Graph 3, p. 49. [m]F. Cortés, Medio Siglo de Desigualdad en México, March 2013, Graph 3 p. 19. [n]Instituto Nacional de Estadística, Geografía e Informática (INEGI), ENIGH Graph 10.1.4, (money income for 2002 only, together with no-money income was reported to be 0.502 in 2016, earlier an adjustment was made for 2015). °F. Cortés y D. Vargas La Evolución de la Desigualdad en México: Viejos y Nuevos Resultados, Graph 3, p. 49. ᵖEl Trimestre Económico, Vol 82, No. 327, 2015 Graph 3, p. 534. ᵠThe complete GINI coefficients, Mexico, 1960-2012. ʳCentro de Estudios de Finanzas Públicas (CEFP) Cámara de Diputados, México, La Pobreza y el Gasto Social 24/6/2019 p. 16. ˢCentro de Estudios de Finanzas Públicas (CEFP) Cámara de Diputados, México, 0009/2008, p. 6. ᵗInstituto Nacional de Estadística, Geografía e Informática (INEGI), Revista Internacional de Estadística y Geografía, (INEGI) Vol. 9 No. special 2018, p. 185. ᵘV. Arámburu, Crecimiento, Pobreza y Desigualdad en México desde una Perspectiva Histórica, El Soberano, August 2019.

Note: All GINI coefficients found in this investigation, which includes a majority of scores published in this matter are represented in the sample scores shown here. Many of these scores use different income base or slightly different methodology, but they are considered proper GINI scores in view of the fact that they use accepted methodology and specify a generally accepted range and average results. In this case most GINI scores shown were found within the range of 0.443 to 0.606, with an average of 0.498 and a median of 0.489. GINI is the preferred world's inequality measurement. A reading of 1.0 refers to a perfectly unequal economic distribution.

Income Distribution

	1950	1963	1957	1968	1977	1984	1989	1992	1994	2000	2010	2015
I y II	4.8	3.5	1.9	3.4	3.9	3.9	3.6	2.3	3.3	4.28	3.6	2.22
III y IV	7.8	6.8	6.2	7.2	7.4	8.9	8.1	7.8	7.6	8.40	8.41	7.27
V y VI	11.0	11.0	11.5	11.6	13.2	14.0	13.0	12.3	12.0	12.0ᵃ	13.4	13.3
VII y VIII	17.5	19.8	20.0	19.6	22.0	22.1	19.4	20.0	19.6	19.1ᵃ	21.4	22.6
IX y X	58.9	58.9	60.5	58.3	54.4	51.20	54.9	56.6	57.5	56.6	53.2	54.5

Souces: Table made up of several studies: Leopoldo Solís. La Realidad Económica Mexicana (modified). p. 341. ᵃIndex Mundi, Mexico Income Distribution, Chart, Income share held by fourth and third highest 20% income. World Economics Association (based on SEDLAC) Inequality in México, Commentaires, Vol 4, Issue 5, October 2014. Ifigenia Martínez and Oscar Altimir en Corbacho & Gerd Schwartz International Monetary Fund (IMF), Working Paper WP/02/12. Miguel del Castillo Negrete R., La Distribución del Ingreso en México, Magazine Este País, 1/4/12. Revista Internacional de Estadística y Geografía, Realidad, Datos y Espacio, Revista, Vol 9, No. Especial, 2018 p. 167.

Income Distribution

	1963	1975	1984	1994
0-10	1.3	0.4	1.9	1.6
11-20	2.2	1.5	3.1	2.7
21-30	3.3	2.5	4.2	3.7
31-40	3.0	3.7	5.2	4.7
41-50	4.9	5.0	6.5	5.7
51-60	6.1	6.5	8.0	7.1
61-70	8.0	8.5	9.9	8.9
71-80	11.8	11.5	12.3	11.4
81-90	17.0	16.9	16.6	16.0
91-100	41.9	43.6	32.4	38.2

Source: Group of Associated Economists based on the Encuesta Nacional de Ingreso-Gasto de los Hogares del Instituto Nacional de Estadística y Geografía (INEGI).

Persons receiving most services (million individuals)

	1960	1980	2000	2010
Trade Union	2.5	2.9	4.7	4.1
Political Party	0.5	1.0	2.2	3.1
Bureaucracy	3.5	5.0	7.0	8.0
Army personnel	0.2	0.2	0.2	0.3
Wealthy people*	1.0	10.5	26.0	28.0
Total	7.7	19.6	40.1	43.5
National Population[a]	37.7	67.7	98.8	114.0
Total Group percent (%)	20.4	28.9	40.5	38.1

Sources: Table created by the author from several sources: Trade Unions, CTM, CROM, CROC, UNT, FAT & NCT, OECD Survey in OECD.Stat; Political Parties, PRI, PAN, PRD, PT, PVE, MC, Morena, See Rice's University Baker Insitute on Foreign Policy in page on Mexican Political Parties; Bureaucracy, FSTSE, ISSSTE, IMSS & Others, Sirvent Gutierrez, Apuntes para el Estudio de la burocracia mexicana, UNAM, Escuela de Ciencias Políticas y Sociales. Zepeda Martinez Disminución de la tasa de trabajadores durnte el periodo neoliberal, Revista de Ciencias Políticas y Sociales UNAM, 51 (2017) Sept/Dic 2009; Army personnel, Mexico, Military strength in Global firepower. *Wealthy people is a residual category since most of them appear classified already in most other sections, it includes private economic sectors and private education organizations, See Gonzalez Ivan, El sector privado como aliado de la Economia Mexicana in NotiPress, 17/02/2020 & La Educación Superior Privada en Mexico, Perfiles Educativos Vol 24 No. 97/98, 2002 in Scielo. [a]World Bank, IBRD, IDA. Data, 2019.

III – Poverty

Poverty in México (percentage of total population)

	Food Poverty	Income Poverty	Property Poverty
1950	61.8	73.2	88.4
1958	61.0	70.0	81.3
1963	45.6	55.9	75.2
1977	25.0	33.0	63.8
1984	22.5	30.2	53.0
1992	22.5	28.0	52.6
1996	37.1	45.3	69.6
2000	24.2	31.9	53.7
2014		45.5*	

Source: Miguel Székely Pobreza y Desigualdad en Mexico entre 1950 y 2004, El Trimestre Económico, vol LXXII (4), No. 288, 2005 pp. 213-231. * World Bank, BIRF, AIF, Data, Pobreza index, Mexico.(Ver Income Distribution Data review in www.oecd.org/social/inequality.htm).

IV – Lack of Competitiveness

Lack of competitiveness of National Industry. Contribution to total supply - 1960

Textil industry	1.8%
Food, Drink & Tobacco	1.8%
Cement	0.7%
Footware	3.7%
Soup	0.01%
Rubber	1.3%
Iron & Steel	17.8%
Paper	39.7%
Fertilizer	68.7%
Auto parts and autos	41.3%
Total Industrias	9.5%

Fuentes: Enrique Cárdenas. La Política Económica en México 1950-1994, p. 69.

Coefficient of import substitution (% constant prices)

	1950	1951	1952	1953	1954	1955	1956	1957	1958	1959	1960
Total	14.40	15.51	21.50	17.12	15.35	14.18	17.05	15.80	11.51	11.27	9.47

Sources: Enrique Cárdenas La Hacienda Pública y la Política Económica 1929-1958. Coefficient of import substitution is calculated as import percentaje from total supply.

Value of Importation subject to prior permit (%).

1983	100	1987	27
1984	83	1988	22
1985	35	1989	20
1986	27		

Source: Leopoldo Solís M. La Realidad Económica Mexicana: Retrovisión y Perspectiva, p. 192

V – Golden Age of Capitalism

Country	Population (millons) 1960	Years	Advance rate (%)	Change (%) 1960-1980	Change (%) 1980-2000
South Korea	25.3	1960-2000	8.7	9.4	8.0
Hong Kong	3.0	1961-2000	7.0	5.6	8.5
Mexico	37.7	1960-2000	4.9	6.7	3.1
Italia	49.7	1960-2000	3.5	4.7	2.2
Ecuador	4.5	1960-2000	3.9	5.5	2.3
Thailand	27.4	1960-2000	6.7	7.2	6.2
Malasia	8.1	1960-2000	7.1	7.7	6.6
Paraguay	1.9	1960-2000	5.1	7.0	3.3
Chile	8.1	1960-2000	4.2	3.7	4.7
Brazil	72.1	1960-2000	4.7	7.4	2.1
Peru	10.1	1960-2000	3.0	4.5	1.6
Spain	30.4	1960-2000	4.2	5.5	2.8

Sources: Macrotrends.net Countries. Historical Data

	Finland	France	Germany	Italy	Spain	Japan	U.S.
Decade 1950	5.0	4.6	7.8	5.2	5.2	9.5	3.2
Decade 1960	5.1	5.8	4.8	7.5	7.5	10.5	4.3

Source: World Bank, BIRF, AIF, Data

Country	Population, 1940 millon	Years	Growth %	GDP 1940	GDP 1950	GDP 1960
Argentina	14.6	1950-1960	2.5	7128	8542	8928
Brazil	41.1	1940-1960	10.4	1115	1549	2280
Mexico	20.2	1940-1960	7.4	1932	2648	3380
Spain	26.0	1940-1960	3.0	4189	4201	5472
Italy	44.4	1940-1960	12.5	3131	3698	7067
South Korea	23.7	1940-1960	2.0	1238	1122	1487
Venezuela	3.4[a]	1940-1960	14.9	2286	4055	5707

Sources: Global Change Data Lab, Economic Growht. Poverty and Economic Development. Global Change Data Lab. Max Roser. Historical series. [a]Estimated population by author.

Evolution of Net Total Expenditures & Public Deficit
(% GDP)

Year	Net Total Expense	Public Deficit
1980	32.5	-5.46
1982	42.2	-15.08
1985	36.7	-7.45
1988	37.6	-10.73
1990	28.5	-2.39
1993	22.8	0.59
1995	23.4	-0.22
1997	23.8	-0.21
2000	22.6	-1.06
2002	24.1	-1.36
2005	21.4[a]	-0.5[b]
2008	23.7[a]	-0.2[b]
2010	25.6[a]	-12.5[b]
2012	24.1[a]	-11.4[b]

Sources: Table based in, Centro de Estudios de Finanzas Públicas (CEFP), Cámara de Diputados CEFP 021/2003 Evolución y Estadísticas del Gasto Público Federal en Mexico 1980-2002, Table, p. IX.[a]Gasto Neto Devengado del Sector Público Presupuestario en Clasificación Administrativa 1980-2012 (Percentage of GDP). [b]Mexicomaxico.org, Ing. Manuel Aguirre B. Balance del Sector Publico Déficit-Superávit Fiscal 1935-2017 (Inclues loses Pidiregas de Pemex). Also, data 1990 Secretaría de Hacienda y Crédito Público (SHCP) Financial situation of the Public sector.

	2007	2008	2009	2010	2011	2012
Budget Income	22.0	23.5	23.8	22.6	21.9	22.1
Budget Expenses	22.0	23.6	26.1	25.5	24.4	25.5
Adjustments	-1.2	-1.0	-2.4	-2.5	-0.5	-0.4

Source: International Monetary Fund (IMF). Data from 2012 are estimates.

Budget (% GDP) Under President Control

Year	thousand pesos[f]	% GDP	Year	thousand pesos[f]	% GDP	Year	thousand pesos[f]	% GDP
1980	683,936	10.87	1985	5,767,289	20.53	1990	58,970,200	16.91
1994	93,360,000	10.91	1995	117,829,700	11.91	1996	1,054,053,000	11.68
2000	1,243,126,600[b]	12.68[c]	2010	3,355,288,000[b]	21.40[c]			

Sources: [a]Instituto de Investigaciones Históricas, Estadísticas Económicas, 4a edition 2013, UNAM. [b]Centro de Estudios de Finanzas Públicas (CEFP), Cámara de Diputados, México, CEFP 020/2012 [c]World Bank, IBRD. IDA, Data, 2019. [f]current pesos. The amounts actually spent were higher, generally bigger before receiving foreign credits, but lower aferwards.

Expenses actualy made (Million pesos)

1940	632	1975	400,725
1945	1,007	1980	910,000
1950	3,463	1985	13,660,000
1955	8,803	1990	156,816,000
1960	20,150	2000	950,427,700
1965	64,020	2005	1,514,918,600
1970	109,201	2010	2,241,831,200

Sources: Instituto de Investigaciones Históricas, Estadísticas Económicas, 4a edition 2013, UNAM pp. 281 & 282.

Budgetary item	1995-2000	2001-2006	2007-2012	2013-2018
Payroll	5.3	3.6	2.5	0.1
Administration	-1.0	8.3	8.4	4.4
Subsidies	-2.5	12.2	9.6	1.7
Investments	-4.1	5.4	16.0	3.0
Pensions	8.9	14.2	9.0	6.6
Unplanned	5.2	2.9	-0.3	7.7

Source: Paulo Cantillo, Newspaper Excelsior 18 January 2020 (Real annual average percentage variation, January-September).

Loans given by FOBAPROA 1994-1998
(Million of pesos)

Serfin	58,064.3	Bancentro	14,062.1	Capital	2,500.0
Banpaís	47,524.4	Unión	12,090.0	Oriente	2,000.0
Inverlat	41,839.5	Atlántico	6,599.3	Sureste	520.0
Confía	26,534.2	Cremi	5,300.0	Interestatal	350.0
Mexicano	24,320.9	Obrero	3,099.0	TOTAL	244,804.3

Sources: Fobaproa. Executive Summary of Operations. Includes only audited Banks and in "special situation" excludes Banamex, Bancomer, Bital, Banorte, Promex, Bancrecer, Probursa (BBV) in Proceso, 40 Años Haciendo Historia Vol 2, 1976-2016.

Households Current Expenditures in México
Mexico's Quarter Current Expenditures in Income Deciles

	Food	Clothing	Housing	Cleaning	Health	Transport	Education	Personal	Transfer
I	50.6	3.8	10.5	6.2	3.2	11.9	5.9	7.0	0.9
II	47.5	3.9	10.9	5.8	2.4	13.5	7.3	7.3	1.3
III	45.1	4.2	10.3	5.6	2.5	14.9	8.6	7.3	1.5
IV	43.1	4.1	10.1	5.2	2.2	16.6	9.8	7.3	1.5
V	41.4	4.2	10.2	5.2	2.3	17.7	9.7	7.2	2.0
VI	39.3	4.4	9.8	5.2	2.5	19.1	10.5	7.2	2.0
VII	35.7	4.7	9.8	5.1	2.3	19.6	11.1	7.2	2.6
VIII	35.6	4.7	9.6	5.2	2.2	20.6	12.0	7.3	2.8
IX	32.4	5.0	9.1	5.5	2.8	21.2	13.2	7.4	3.4
X	25.2	5.0	7.3	7.3	3.3	21.5	17.0	7.7	4.5

Sources: Table based in: Centro de Estudios de Finanzas Públicas (CEFP) La Pobreza y el Gasto Social en México, 2016, data from Instituto Nacional de Estadísticas y Geografía (INEGI). Encuesta Nacional de Ingresos y Gastos de los Hogares (ENIGH), 2016 (24 june 2019).

Public Expenditures in Social Development 1990-2019A

(% from total expenses in Social Development) Year	1990	2000	2010	2015	2016	2017	2018	2019[a]
Education	40.7	39.9	33.3	25.4	24.8	25.0	24.0	22.7
Health Care	45.5	23.5	24.1	18.4	18.0	19.3	18.6	18.1
Housing & Community Services	9.7	10.3	11.4	12.2	11.4	7.1	7.3	7.2
Social Potection	1.6	23.8	22.9	41.9	43.7	47.2	48.6	50.9
Other	2.5	2.6	8.0	--	--	--	--	--
Entertainment	--	--	--	1.0	0.8	0.7	0.7	0.6
Environmental Protection	--	--	--	1.0	0.9	0.7	0.7	0.5

Sources: Centro de Estudios de las Finanzas Públicas (CEFP), LaPobreza y el Gasto Social 2016, Cámara de Diputados, June 24, 2019. [a]Provisional statistics.

	Urban Population[a]		Enrollment Superior Education[c]	Superior Education Schools	Expense Private Health[d]	
	Millions	%[b]			Pesos, Millions	%[c]
1970	25.17	48.9	271,275	366[g]	--	--
1990	59.83	71.3	1,252,027	1,238[g]	539,789,025	59.56
2000	73.81	74.7	2,047,895	4,049[h]	366,023,424	54.78

2005	80.89	76.3	2,538,256	5,116[h]	516,985,337	57.76
2008	85.54	77.2	2,705,190[h]	5,560[h]	480,538,335	54.09
2010	88.79	79.2	2,981,313	6,289[h]	490,325,939	47.83
2015	96.56	79.2	3,648,945	7,057[h]	547,533,097	47.83
2018	99.69	79.9	3,943,544	--	586,357,172[f]	48.52
2019	102.57	80.4	4,561,972[h]	6,359[i]	--	--

Sources: Table based in data from World Inequality Data Base (WID). [a]Instituto Nacional de Geografía, Estadística e Informática (INEGI). [b] Percentage of total population. [c]Revista Latinoamericana de Estudios Educativos Vol XLIII, No. 3, 2013, Chart 5 p. 84. [d]Jose B Ramirez, El Colegio de la Frontera Norte, Costos de los Servicios de Salud, 2012. Sesma-Vasquez, Perez-Rico y otros Gasto Privado en Salud, Salud Publica, 2018. [e]Total percentage of Health expenditures. [f]Secretaría de Salud, Sistema de Información. [g]Salinas de Gortari, Las Políticas Sociales de México en los Años Noventa (1993a). [h]SEP, tables without label. [i]DGESU Dirección General de Educación Superior Universitaria, SEP. Expansión Datosmacro.com Mexico, Economía y Demografía.

Social Public Expenditure in México % GDP (1990-2000)
(Includes expenditure in Poverty, Health & Education)

1990	1991	1992	1993	1994	1995	1996	1997	1998	1999	2000
6.0	7.0	7.8	8.4	9.2	8.4	8.3	8.6	9.0	9.4	9.4

2005[a]	2006[a]	2007[a]	2008[a]	2009[a]	2010[a]	2011[a]	2012[a]	2013[a]	2014[a]	2016[a]
8.6	8.3	8.8	9.2	10.6	10.6	10.3	10.6	11.1	11.9	11.6

Sources: Centro de Estudios de las Finanzas Públicas (CEFP), CEFP 049/2006, Participación del Gasto Programable del Sector Público Presupuestario en Clasificación Funcional en el PIB 1990-2002, p. 65. [a]Nota Informativa notacefp 007/2016. El Gasto Público Federal en el Desarrollo Económico y Social de Mexico, written by the Centro de Estudios de las Finanzas Públicas (CEFP) based in sources of the Secretaría de Hacienda y Crédito Público (SHCP), 28 march 2016.

	1940	1950	1955	1960	1965	1970	1980	2000	2010	2015	2018
Social Expense Mill. USD	29	256	597	1885	4,074	7,817	--	10,39[f]	13,282	18,074	
% GDP	--	--	--	--	--	--	8.6[a]	6.26[b]	9.64[b]	10.49[b]	7.5[c]

Sources: [a]Cuadernos CEPAL, Diciembre 1994. [b]Cepal-ONU Portal de Inversión social. [c]Organisation for Economic Co-operation and Development. (OECD) Public Social Expense, 2018. [f]Constant pesos 2003.

Social Public Expenditures % GDP

	1990-91	1994-95	2000-01	2005-06
Latinoamérica	12.9	14.9	15.7	15.9
Mexico	6.5	8.9	9.7	10.2

Source: Comisión Económica Para América Latina y el Caribe (CEPAL),Panorama Social de América Latina. Santiago de Chile, 2008, pp. 136 & 137.

Benefits Package of Social Security in Mexico (Instituto Mexicano del Seguro Social, IMSS)
1. Health Insurance 2. Disability Insurance 3. Occupational risk Insurance 4. Life Insurance 5. Day care for of workers' children 6. Sports and Cultural Center 7. Retirement pension 8. Housing credits.

Benefits of Social Protection in México (Instituto Mexicano del Seguro Social, IMSS).
1. Health services given by federal and state entities other than IMSS. 2. Subsidies for housing by federal programs and entities other than Infonavit. 3. Access to savings pensions to be able to withdrew in personal accounts. 4. Access to day care from federal and state programs other than IMSS. 5. Access to life insurance related to some health services.

Source: Levy, 2008. Good Intentions, bad outcomes: Social Policy, Informality and Growth in Mexico. The Brookings Institution, 2008.

VIII - Education

Population Education 1960-2010
(older than 15 years of age)

	No school at all	Primary Incomplete	Primary Complete	Secondary Incomplete	Secondary Complete	Senior High	Superior
1960	40.1	40.3	12	2.4	2.1	2.1	1
1970	31.6	38.9	16.8	3.4	3	3.9	2.4
1980	13.7	23.2	19.7	6.3	14	14.6	8.5
1990	10.3	18.1	19.4	5.3	19.1	16.8	11.0
2000	8.5	14.6	17.9	4.9	21.5	19.5	13.1
2010	6.9	11.1	18.5	4.2	23.9	20.7	14.7

Source: Aleida Azamar A. El Modelo Educativo Mexicano. Una Historia en Construcción. Development by the author with data from the Sistema de Educación Nacional (SEN) y del Instituto Nacional de Geografía y Estadística (INEGI). Bachillerato includes Education School, College and Post-graduate studies.

Note: The School System in Mexico includes Elementary school (6 years), Secondary school (3 years) Preparatory scool (3 years), Professional Studies or College (usually 5 years), and Post-graduate (2 or 3 years).

Years of School for Students 25 & 34 years of age 1970, 1990, 2000 & 2005

Total	1970	1990	2000	2005
Promedio	3.6	7.2	8.8	9.4
Porcentil X	0	1	3	4

Porcentil XXV	0	4	6	6
Porcentil L	3	6	9	9
Porcentil LXXV	6	9	12	12
Porcentil XC	8	15	16	16

Sources: Development by the author based on survey of the Instituto Nacional de Geografía y Estadística (INEGI) in Patricio Solís, La desigualdad de Oportunidades y las Brechas deEscolaridad, El Colegio de México, 2010.

	1940	1950	1960	1970	1980	1990	1994	2000
Average Formal years of Education (Total población)	1.7	2.1	2.8	3.7	5.4	6.3	6.6	7.6[a]

Sources: Nora C Lustig & Miguel Székely. México Evolución Económica, Pobreza y Desigualdad. Chart 2. Indicadores de Bienestar Social 1940-1994 p. 28. For the year 2000 was used the [a]Table of the Instituto para la Evaluación Educativa (INEE) CS3Oa Tabla de Escolaridad Media de la Población de 15 años o más.

School Cycle 1963-64

Level	Students		Schools		Teachers	
	No.	%	No.	%	No.	%
Pre-school	283 778	3.8	2 208	5.6	8 130	4.0
Primary	6 470 110	87.7	35 038	89.3	135 798	66.8
Secondary	388 551	5.3	1 427	3.6	29 565	14.5
Senior High	140 174	1.9	417	1.1	16 650	8.2
Superior	97 157	1.3	134	0.3	13 200	6.5
Preparation to work	0	0.0	0	0.0	0	0.0
Total	7 379 770	100.0	39 224	100.0	203 343	100.0

School Cycle 2011-12

Level	Students		Schools		Teachers	
	No.	%	No.	%	No.	%
Pre-school	4 705 545	13.5	91 253	35.7	224 146	12.1
Primary	14 909 419	42.7	99 378	38.9	573 849	30.9
Secondary	6 167 424	17.7	36 563	14.3	388 769	20.9
Senior High	4 333 589	12.4	15 427	6.0	285 974	15.4
Superior	3 161 195	9.1	6 878	2.7	342 269	18.4
Preparation to work	1 614 327	4.6	5 999	2.3	41 222	2.2
Total	34 891 499	100.0	255 498	100.0	1 856 229	100.0

Sources: Revista Latinoamericana de Estudios Educativos Vol XLIII No. 3, 2013. Own development of this magazine based on Statistics of the Secretaría de Educación Pública (SEP),

2013a and 1013b. College & Post-grad. includes Education in Education school, College and Post-graduate school.

Evolution and structure of the public expenditures in Education (2004-2010)
(Millions of pesos, 2010)

	2004	%	2006	%	2008	%	2010	%
Education-Total	391,930	43.1	417,528	41.6	452,50	40.2	456,643	38.1
Basic	267,594	29.4	286,659	28.5	306,06	27.2	299,482	25.0
Senior High	42,603	4.7	44,716	4.5	46,04	4.1	48,207	4.0
Superior	56,664	6.2	58,499	5.8	71,38	6.3	76,951	6.4
Post-grad	5,094	0.6	4,896	0.5	5,033	0.4	4,931	0.4
Gov. Scholarship	3,046	0.3	3,117	0.3	4,82	0.4	5,937	0.5
Other Scholarship	16,930	1.9	19,642	2.0	19,125	1.7	21,135	1.8
GDP expense		4.7		4.7		4.8		5.1

Sources: Secretaría de Hacienda y Crédito Público (SHCP). Distribución del Pago de Impuestos y Recepción del Gasto Público por Deciles de Hogares y Personas, 2010, Table 3.1 p. 50. *Datos del Banco Mundial, BIRF, AIF, Gasto Público en Educación, México, 2016.

1994
Family expenses-Education
Income Deciles

	Households	Total expenses	Cumulated
I	13.2	0.8	0.4
II	18.4	1.0	1.3
III	25.4	1.5	2.9
IV	25.6	1.7	5.0
V	30.4	1.7	7.7
VI	28.6	1.9	11.4
VII	34.0	2.4	16.9
VIII	38.1	3.1	25.6
IX	45.0	3.2	38.2
X	53.3	7.5	100.0

2000
Family expenses-Education
Income Deciles

	Households	Total expenses	Cumulated
I	15.0	1.8	0.4
II	28.1	3.0	1.6

III	29.9	3.8	3.3
IV	37.1	4.3	5.8
V	41.1	4.9	9.1
VI	46.9	6.1	14.1
VII	42.2	6.5	20.2
VIII	51.5	7.1	28.6
IX	59.5	9.8	43.7
X	68.6	18.2	100.0

Source: Ana Corbacho y Gerd Schwartz, Mexico: Experiences with Pro-Poor Expenditure Policies, International Monetary Fund (IMF), WP/02/12, p. 26. Table modified by the authors.

Percentage Teacher/student

Students	1950	1956	1960	1965	1970	1975	1980	1985
Teachers	35.12	32.64	33.66	35.14	34.80	31.55	29.58	25.56

Source: [a]IMF, Corbacho & Gerd Schwartz, International Monetary Fund (IMF), Working Paper WP/02/12, pp. 20 & 21.

IX – Health Care

Total expense on Health care in Mexico as percentage of GDP (includes public and private expenditure)

1995	5.0	2003	6.0	2012	5.8	2018	5.46
1998	5.5	2004	6.4	2013	5.9		
1999	5.6	2008	--	2014	5.6		
2000	5.6	2009	--	2015	5.7		
2001	6.0	2010	5.9	2016	5.4		
2002	6.0	2011	5.7	2017	5.5		

Source: Instituto Nacional de Geografía y Estadísticas (INEGI).

Health expenditures vs. GDP

	1998	1999	2000	2001	2002	2003	2004
Public expense	2.5	2.9	3.0	2.7	2.7	2.8	3.1
Private expense	2.9	2.7	2.6	3.3	3.3	3.2	3.3
Total	5.4	5.6	5.6	6.0	6.0	6.0	6.4

Sources: Instituto Nacional de Geografía y Estadísticas (INEGI). Estadísticas Asociación Mexicana de Instituciones de Seguros (AMIS), en Milliman. Health Insurance in Mexico: Factors to Drive its Growth, p. 8.

	Expenses Health[a] GDP 1996-2004		
	%	Public %	Private %
1996	5.1	2.3	2.8
1998	5.6	2.6	3.0
1999	5.5	2.9	2.5
2000	5.6	2.6	3.0
2004	6.4	3.1	3.3

Source: [a]Secretaría de Salud, Sistema de Información.

Population with legal access to health service 2000 & 2005
(Thousands of persons)

Coverage	2000		2005
IMSS	31,523		32,088
PEMEX, Defense, Navy	2,098		1,085
ISSSTE	5,782		5,750
Popular Insurance	--		7,321
Private Insurance	--		1,898
Other	--		1,051
Non specified	2,807		3,048
Uninsured	55,304		55,633

Sources: Censo Nacional de Población y Vivienda 2000 y Conteo de Población y Vivienda 2005, Instituto Nacional de Geografía y Estadísticas (INEGI) in Ethos Fundation. El Seguro Popular en México: Posibles efectos sobre la economía informal. February 2011. Graph 1, p. 19.

X – Migration to the Cities

	Mexico Total Population		Mexico Rural Population	
	(Millions)		(Millions)	(%)
	INEGI[c]		INEGI[e]	f
1940	19.6		12.8	65.30
1950	25.7		14.8	57.58
1960	34.9		17.2	35.68
1970	48.2		19.9	51.02
1980	66.8		22.5	33.70
1990	81.2		23.3	28.69
1995	91.2		24.2	26.53

2000	97.4		24.7	25.35
2005	103.2		24.3	23.54
2010	112.3		24.9	23.15
2015	119.9		27.4	22.93

Sources: [c]Instituto Nacional de Estadística, Geografía e Informática (INEGI), Population and Housing Census. Data census survey 2009, 2011, 2015, 2016. [e]Totals based on official data from Instituto Nacional de Estadística, Geografía e Informática (INEGI). [f]Percentage of rural population.

Note: Population statistics from World Bank are greater than those based on domestic sources, for 2015 total population was 121,858,258 unhabitants according to this organization.

Mexico: Domestic Migration 1921-2010

Year	Population	Migrants	%
1921	14,334,780	1,189,606	8.30
1930	16,552,722	1,688,930	10.20
1940	19,653.552	2,081,193	10.59
1950	25,779,254	3,305,117	12.82
1960	34,923,129	5,008,697	14.34
1970	48,225,238	6,984,483	14.48
1980	66,846,833	11,245,100	16.82
1990	82,249,645	13,963,020	17.19
2000	97,487,412	17,220,424	17.66
2010	112,336,538	19,747,511	17.58

Source: Jaime Sobrino, La Migración Interna en México en la Primera Década del Nuevo Milenio, Chart 1. Domestic Migración, 1900-2010, p. 204

Year	Urban Population		CO₂ Emissions[c]	Private National Credit		Subscription Phone Celular
	millons[a]	%[b]	(metric tons)	Students[d]	% GDP[e]	(100s)[f]
2017	99.65	79.8	3.93[g]	14,020,204	35.32	91,627
2016	98.14	79.5	3.89[g]	14,137,862	34.00	90,592
2015	96.61	79.2	4,000	14,250,425	31.95	88,372
2010	88.78	77.8	4,070	14,887,845	23.32	80,096
2000	73.89	74.7	4,028	14,792,528	15.04	14,234
1990	59.95	71.4	3,793	14,401,588	17.55	76
1980	44.95	66.3	3,962	14,666,257[i]	18.35	0
1970	30.39	59.0	2,215	9,248,190[i]	32,93	0
1960	19.17	50.7	1,671	5,342,092[i]	20,61	0
1950	10.90	42.4	60[h]	2,997,054[i]	--	--
1940	6.80	34.6	20[h]	1,960,755[i]	--	--

Sources: [a]Macrotrends, Urban Population in Mexico. Jaime Sobrino, La urbanización en el México contemporáneo. Notas de Población No. 94, ONU Comisión Económica para América Latina y el Caribe (CEPAL). [b]Porcentaje del total de la población. [c]World Bank, IBRD, IDA, Data in metric tons per cápita. [d]Dirección General de Estadística, Anuario Estadístico, Celerino Cano, La Acción Cultural y Educación de México, en Historia de la Educación de México, 1981. [i]Estadísticas SEP. [e]International Monetary Fund (IMF), internal Credit. [f]International Monetary Fund (FMI) cellular phone subsription. [g]datosmacro.com Mexico-Emissions of CO_2 [h]N. Onhe, J. Fuglstvedt, H. Blum & R Bieltevedt, Contributions of Individual Countries's Emissions to climate Change and their Uncertainties, total output.

Total Students of the National School System 1950-2000 (In thousand of students)

1950	1960	1970	1980	1990	1997	1998	1999	2000
3,249.2	5,941.5	11,538.9	21,464.9	25,092.0	28,094.3	28,618.0	29,151.5	29,668.8[a]

Source: En El Perfil de la Educación en México, Secretaría de Educación Pública, 1997, p. 10. [a]Estimated year.

XI - Informal Economy.

Informal Economy in México

	2000	2001	2002	2003	2004	2005	2006
Informality worker sector	27.0	27.5	28.2	28.3	28.8	28.1	27.1
Non registered percentage	57.6	57.5	57.2	57.2	57.5	58.9	60.1
% of Population Informal workers	42.2	42.4	42.4	42.5	42.7	40.4	39.5

	2007	2008	2009	2010	
Informality worker sector	27.0	27.3	28.2	28.7	
Non registered percentage	60.7	61.7	61.2	61.4	
% of Population Informal workers	39.2	36.7	39.2	39.0	

Sources: Data from Instituto Nacional de Geografía y Estadística (INEGI). Includes calculations from Ethos using data from Encuesta Nacional de Empleo y Encuesta Nacional de Ocupación y Empleo. Ethos Fundación. El Seguro Popular en México: Posibles efectos sobre la economía informal. Febrero de 2011. Chart 2 p. 30.

Informality Rate

1990	55.5		1994	57.0		1996	60.2		2008	55.5[a]	

Source: From Enrique Hernandez Laos. Crecimiento, Distribución y Pobreza Revistas UNAM, Economía UNAM Vol 6, No. 16, 2009, p. 49 . Wide interpretation from workers outside the law. [a]Estimate from Hernández Laos for 2008.

XII – Corruption

Cause of Corruption by Level of Education

	Total		Primary		Secondary		College
Lack of law enforcement	14		15		14		15
Culture/Education	44		26		40		55
Need	18		24		21		12
Transparency	7		4		8		6
Lack of supervisión	12		21		13		8
Other	3		6		2		4
No answer	2		4		2		1
Total	100		100		100		100

Sources: J Bailey & P Paras, Perceptions and Attitudes about Corruption and Democracy in Mexico in Mexican Studies, Tabla 3 p. 66.

México's Rate of World Corruption (Rank)

2010		2012		2016		2018		2019
98		105		123		138		130

Source: Trading Economics 2020, Mexico Corruption Index.

Index of Perception of Corruption.

1995	1996	1997	1998	1999	2000	2001	2002	2003	2004	2005	2006
31	33	26	33	34	33	37	36	36	36	35	33

2007	2008	2009	2010	2011	2012	2013	2014	2015	2016
35	36	33	31	30	34	34	35	35	30

Sources: Transparencia Internacional 1995-2016. The Index of Perception of Corruption changed and simplified its metodology in 2012, therefore it is not possible to make strict comparisons with prior years to this date. In addition, starting this year, the scale of measurement (which was from 0 to 10) is from 0 to 100.

XIII – Economic Performance of the Presidents from National Action Party (PAN) 2000-2012

	2000	2001	2002	2003	2004	2005	2006	Promedio
Vicente Fox 2001-2006	6.6	-0.6	0.8	1.4	4.2	2.8	4.8	2.89[a]
	2007	2008	2009	2010	2011	2012	2013	
Felipe Calderón 2007-2012	4.8	3.3	1.8	-6.5	3.9[b]	2.3[b]	4.4[b]	0.19[a]

Sources: A Terrones c., Y. Sanchez T., JR Vargas S., Crecimiento Económico y Crisis en México, 1970-2009 Un Análisis Sexenal, pp. 9 & 10. [a]A. Aparicio Cabrera, Economía Mexicana 1910-2010: Balance de un Siglo, UNAM 2010, Chart 3, p. 14. [b]Datos Banco Mundial, BIRF AIF Crecimiento del PIB (% Annual), Mexico.

	1980-2000	2000-2012
Average growth GDP	0.8	0.9
Total growth	17.2	10.4
Average growth GDP		
Latin-America	0.3	0.9
Total growth	5.7	22.8

Sources: Fondo Monetario Internacional (FMI). Weisbrot Mark & Ray Rebecca The Scorecard on Development 1960-2010. Closing the Gap? Center for Economic and Policy Research (CEPR) and United Nations Department of Economic and Social Affairs (DESA). Working Paper No. 106, 2012.

Year	Urban Population[a] (millions)	%[b]	Homicide Criminal[c]	Vehicles registered Country[d] (millions)	Año	Informal Economy GDP[e] %	Immigrants to U.S.[f]
1980	40.84	60.3	12,225	5,758.3	2003	23.6	2,199,200
1990	59,83	71.3	14,497	9,862.1	2010	23.5	4,298,000
2000	73,81	74.7	13,849	15,611.9	2015	22.8	9,177,500
2010	88,79	79.2	20,680	32,338.8	2016	22.6	11,711,000
2015	96,56	79.2	17,034	39,975.9	2017	22.6	11,279.900
2018	99,69	79.9	28,816	47,790.9	2018	22.5	12,300,000

Sources: Chart by author, among others, [a] Instituto Nacional de Estadística, Geografía e Informática (INEGI), Estadísticas Históricas de Mexico, 2014, Population. [b]Percentage of total population. [c]Mexicomaxico,org Economía Mexicana, México 2011. [d]Instituto Naciona de Estadística, Geografía e Informática (INEGI), Parque vehicular, Total Nacional de vehículos, Eduardo M Moctezuma Estudio de Motorización en México, pág. 25. [e]Instituto Naciona de Estadística, Geografía e Informática (INEGI). Medición de la Economía Informal, base 2013. [f]US Census Bureau 2010 y 2017.

Year	GDP[a] (thousand million)	Population (thousand)[b]	Popular Ins.[c] (thousand.)	Complaint Bus. theft (thousand)	Complaint Extorsion[d] (thousand)	Homicide rate (100,000 people)
2000	707,907	98.8998	--	54.21	1.19	13.8
2005	877,476	106.0052	11.4	50.81	2.86	10.6
2009	900,045	112.4638	31.1	63.32	5.88	19.8
2010	1,058,000	114.0929	40.0	70.25	5.63	18.5
2011	1,180,000	115.6954		72.31	4.60	20.0
2013	1,274,000	118.8271	34.7[e]			23.0

Sources: [a]Data World Bank BIRD AIF, Mexico. [b]Data World Bank BIRD AIF, Mexico.[c]El Seguro Popular en México: Posibles efectos sobre la Economía Informal, Febrero 2011, p. 40. [d]G Robles, G Calderon, B. Magaloni, Las Consecuencias Económicas de la Violencia del Narcotráfico en México, Secretariado Ejecutivo Nacional del Sistema de Seguridad Pública,

Inter-American Development Bank (BID), 2013, p. 19. ^cInstituto Nacional de Geografía y
Estadística (INEGI), Comunicado de Prensa, 668/18 December 2018.

Children less than 15 years old treated for leukemia by the Government 2004-2012.

Year	Treated by Gov. facility	Treated by Social Security	Total
2004	4,611	4,755	9,366
2005	5,953	4,248	10,201
2006	7,213	4,633	11,846
2007	9,416	4,671	14,087
2008	10,301	4,728	15,029
2009	11,146	4,891	16,037
2010	10,737	5,206	15,943
2011	11,889	5,286	17,175
2012	13,644	5,646	19,290
Total	84,910	44,064	128,974

Source: R. Lozano F Garrido, World Health Organization (WHO), Mexico, Catastrophic
Health Insurance Fund, 2015 p. 20.

XIV – Economic Performance of President Peña Nieto (PRI), 2013-2018

	2014	2015	2016	2017	2018
GDP Annual rate%	2.8	3.3	2.9	2.1	2.1
GDP per capita	10,954	9,654	8,804	9,379	9,791
Industrial Production (Change%)	2.6	1.2	0.4	-0.2	0.5
Inflation rate (Annual change %)	4.0	2.7	2.8	6.0	4.9
Foreign debt (% GDP)	32.5	35.6	38.3	37.7	36.6
Current account (% GDP)	-1.9	-2.6	-2.2	-1.7	-1.8
International reserves (US dlrs)	32.5	35.6	38.3	37.7	36.6
Exchange rate Peso/US dlrs	13.1	14.82	17.35	20.73	19.86
Importation Gasoline (thousand daily barrels)[a]	370.5	427.1	505.1	570.6	--

Fuentes: [a]A. Jósefowicz Balance de la Economía Mexicana en el Sexenio de Peña Nieto 2000-
2006, Argentina, 2019.. Focus Economics, Barcelona, España, Abril 21,2020 en focus-
economics.com.

Homicides during Peña Nieto period
(homicidies for 100,000 inhabitants)

2009	2010	2011	2012	2013	2014	2015	2016	2017	2018	2019
18	23	24	22	19	17	17	20	26	29	14

Source: Statista, M. Pascuali, Mexico: Murder rate 2009-2019, marzo 2, 2020.

XV – Other Economic Data From Foreign Countries

	GDP (1980-2000)	US	China	SouthCorea	Vietnam	Chile	Costa Rica
Agriculture	1.3	3.8	5.0	2.5	4.6	3.7	5.6
Industry	2.5	3.2	12.4	8.9	--	4.8	4.5
Manufacture	3.0	3.4	12.3	9.8	--	4.0	4.9
Services	2.2	3.0	11.3	7.1	--	4.3	4.0
Total	2.1	3.1	10.2	7.3	6.3	5.5	4.2

Source: International Monetary Fund (IMF). David Ibarra. Ensayos sobre Economía Mexicana, p. 97

Australia

Population	2006	2007	2008	2009	2010	2011	2012	2013	2014
Population	20,697	21,016	21,384	21,779	22,065	22,324	22,684	22,976	23,480[a]
GDP	3.7	3.7	1.7	1.9	2.3	3.7	2.5	2.5	2.7
GDP per capita	37,582	39,342	39,703	41,148	42,253	43,801	43,675	44,706	44,971
Inflation (CPI)	3.5	2.3	4.3	1.7	2.9	3.3	1.7	2.4	2.4

Canada

Population	32,576	32,927	33,317	33,726	34,126	34,483	34,880	35,317	35.440[a]
GDP	2.6	2.0	1.1	-2.7	3.3	2.9	1.9	2.0	2.4
GDP per capita	37,822	39,226	40,108	38,709	40,055	41,56	42,28	43,038	44,057
Inflation (CPI)	2.0	2.1	2.3	0.2	1.7	2.9	1.5	0.9	1.9

Brazil

Population	185,56	187,64	189,61	191,48	193,25	194,93	196,52	198,04	202,800[a]
GDP	4.0	6.0	5.0	-0.2	7.5	3.9	1.9[b]	3.0[b]	0.5[a]
GDP per capita	11,434	12,365	13,160	13,113	14,178	15,065	12,370	12300	12,113
Inflation (CPI)	4.1	3.6	5.6	4.8	5.0	6.6	5.4	6.2	6.3

Chile

Population	16,432	16,598	16,763	16,928	17,094	17,248	17,402	17,556	17,760[a]
GDP	5.6	5.1	3.2	1.3	5.7	5.	5.	4.2	1.8
GDP per capita	15,496	16,708	16,326	16,135	18,172	20,188	21.108	21,888	22,253
Inflation (CPI)	3.3	4.4	8.7	0.3	1.4	3.3	3.0	1.7	4.7

France

Population	61,597	61,995	62,300	62,615	62,917	63,224	63,519	63,794	66,130[a]
GDP	2.3	2.3	0.1	-2.9	1.9	2.0	0.1	0.6	0.1
GDP per capita	32,311	34,064	35,169	34,836	35,896	37,353	37,281	37,617	38,869
Inflation (CPI)	1.6	1.4	2.8	0.0	1.5	2.1	1.9	0.8	0.5

Japan

Population	127,77	127,77	127,69	127,51	128,05	127,79	127,51	127,24	127,30[a]
GDP	1.6	2.1	-1.0	-5.5	4.6	-0.4	1.7	1.6	-0.1
GDP per capita	31,794	33,319	33,499	31,860	33,747	34,312	35,600	36,224	36,455
Inflation (CPI)	0.2	0.0	1.3	-1.3	-0.7	-0.2	-0.0	0.3	2.7

Spain

Population	44,116	44,878	45,555	45,908	46,070	46,174	46,146	46,046	46.510[a]
GDP	4.1	3.7	1.1	-3.5	0.0	1.0	-2.6	-1.6	1.3
GDP per capita	30,905	32,800	33,708	32,803	32,360	32,534	32,392	32,546	33,168
Inflation (CPI)	3.5	2.7	4.0	-0.2	1.7	3.1	2.4	1.4	-0.1

Mexico

Population	108,40	109,18	111,29	112,85	114,25	115,68	117,05	118,39	120.40[a]
GDP	4.9	3.2	1.3	-4.7	5.1	3.9	4.0	1.4	2.1
GDP per capita	13,504	14,131	14,743	14,394	14,139	16,366	16,808	16,891	17,830
Inflation (CPI)	3.6	3.9	5.1	5.2	4.1	3.4	4.1	3.8	4.0

Sources: Organization for Economic Cooperation and Developmente (OECD) in OECD. Stat Also Eurostat, especially [a]Instituto Nacional de Estadísticas y Estudios Económicos (INSEE) francés.